Faith in Abertillery

A twofold love story

A novella by Tracy Traynor

Special thanks go to my good friend Nigel, whose help with editing and storyline has been, as always, invaluable.

Book cover designed by Sharon Clare http://sharonclare.com

Table of Contents

Foreword...3

Chapter 1 4

Chapter 2...8

Chapter 3..19

Chapter 4 29

Chapter 5..44

Chapter 6..54

Chapter 7..64

Chapter 8..75

Chapter 9..85

Chapter 10 96

Chapter 11 108

Chapter 12 123

Chapter 13 126

Chapter 14 138

Chapter 15 148

Chapter 16 160

Chapter 17..174

Chapter 18 182

Chapter 19 190

Chapter 20..198

Thank you so much for reading Faith in Abertillery. 203

The Welsh Revival..204

Research Sources..206

Glossary of Welsh Words...207

Foreword

Dear Readers

The reason for using the American version of spelling is because the majority of my sales are in the US. Dearest English-Readers, please skip over the words such as endeavor and woolen that may cause you to think I don't know how to spell.

I've attempted to capture the beautiful Musicality of the Welsh language and the way the Welsh speak, so please allow for this if you are a hot-shot with grammar and accents. There has been a certain amount of debate on whether to include Welsh words or not. Conflicting advice has come in regarding words used in the North and South of Wales, and sayings that relate to different eras of time. I've realized that whatever I do, I will no doubt cause someone to declare... well that's not right!

Having given it much thought I have decided that I am going to base my Welsh sayings on two things: 1) A plethora of newspaper articles I read from the Welsh archives, which give reports of the day back in 1904/1905 which can't be denied as being accurate accounting of events. 2) Two books that I read during my research. Both are novels written by Welsh people who lived in South Wales during the early 1900s, and so wrote from their experience. I trust the words they included in their stories to be true accounts of language in 1905, in South Wales. Glossary of Welsh words used at the end of the book.

I've tried my hardest to portray an accurate way of talking in Wales in 1905, but as I'm not Welsh, and was born in 1961, not everything may be perfect. It is, however, written with much love, and with the hope that you will thoroughly enjoy the story as you take a glimpse into Welsh history with me.

Chapter 1

Just after eleven o'clock on a February evening in 1905, a solo voice rings out with the hymn 'Here is love vast as the ocean.' Maybe a thousand people are crammed into Ebenezer Baptist Church, in Abertillery. Leaning over the gallery, squashed amongst the bodies of mostly well-built miners, is a skinny young redhead called Faith, attending this evening's service simply to find out what all the ballyhoo's about.

Expectant silence captivates as a miner's voice fills the church, "Loving kindness as the flood." Goose bumps prickle along Faith's arms and the hairs on the back of her neck stand on end. The voice, rich and deep, resonates throughout the church, carrying the man's convictions with powerful intensity. Moved beyond explanation, tears trickle down her cheeks. Glancing at the surrounding people she finds lots of them crying unashamedly, their faces impassioned with love.

During the third line of the hymn, "When the Prince of Life, our Ransom," the congregation joins in. Vibrant sound rises and erupts, filling the church with explosive tension as people fling their hearts into worship. Convinced it's the sound angels would make, Faith takes a timorous peek at the wooden rafters, half expecting an angelic presence. Her atheist life knows nothing of God or religion. In fact, she believes that if there is a God, then at birth He'd seen her defects and cast her aside without mercy. *What am I doing here?* Sorrow clings to her persona, like limpets to a stone. *I'm too wicked for this place.* Desperate need to escape the atmosphere of love makes her spin around and start pushing her way towards the exit. It's slow going. People eager to see the front of the church are straining forward in their praise. Most of them, caught in their own rhapsody, don't even realize she's trying to leave. Living her worst nightmare where moving forward is impossibly difficult, like wading through mud, fear makes her shudder. Realizing, just like her night terrors, that someone is after her.

"Let me through," she wails, her flailing arms knocking anyone close. Eventually a gap opens, and she's able to stumble her way towards the door.

"Ew all right, girl?" a notably plump, yet kindly woman inquires.

Faith's eyes are wide with distress, she moves past the woman not registering what she's asked. Instead, all she observes is the overly tall, flower-pot hat on the woman's head, which brims over with black, crushed-silk roses. Funeral hat, Faith thinks, continuing to push her way forward.

With relief, she reaches the narrow wooden stairwell. In her haste, she trips and starts to fall down the last few stairs. The awful feeling of falling rushes from her feet to her head, and panic tosses bile into her stomach. Disaster is averted when strong arms catch her and bring her safely to the ground. Glancing up to regard her savior, she locks onto the warmest pair of sea-blue eyes she's ever encountered.

The man who holds her by her elbows gazes back for a moment, before letting her go. "I ran out the first time I was touched. You should stay though, there is great peace here."

With a quick glance Faith gauges he's a toff. More obvious than his immaculate attire is his air of self-assured arrogance. Oh, she knows all about his type. Before stopping to think, she sticks her tongue out at him, and rushes through the doorway.

Cold air engulfs her. Regret at leaving is instant, although she's not sure why. She feels vacant and detached. Icy wisps of wind caresses her face, flicking her long hair into the air. Yet it isn't the cold making her shiver. It's the sudden knowledge she's just left something precious behind. This feeling of loss emphasizes her emptiness and solitude.

Instead of taking the path home she tiptoes alongside the church wall, tracing her fingers against the austere brickwork in the dark. The words of the second verse filter through the building. As she leans her head against the freezing wall the words 'Heaven's peace and perfect justice, kissed a guilty world in love' pulsates from the building.

Pain grips in spasms causing her to crumple upon the damp grass, as a hidden compartment within her soul cracks open. Groans carry the anguish of squashed rejection. Skirt and underskirts billow around her, forming a sea of brown ruffles. Wrapping her arms around her body, she tries to stay the waves of nauseating pain. The tightly fitted jacket buttoned up to her neck does nothing to stem the cold or agony.

Suddenly, she is nudged out of her grieving bubble as a heavy coat encases her shoulders. She doesn't need to look up to see who it is, for the slight smell of musky cologne tells her the coat belongs to the man with the deep blue eyes.

"Here."

Faith is grateful for the soft cotton handkerchief he passes her, and wipes her face with gentle dabs. After a moment, she puts her hand against the wall and pushes herself up.

"Thank you." Her voice is halting, her gaze cast downwards.

"Come, let me walk you home."

"No." Faith's head snaps up. Looking at him, she doesn't care that her face will no doubt be red and blotchy. "Thank you for your kindness." Shrugging off the coat she hands it back to him. "I can see myself home."

Taking the coat he watches as she marches, with a somewhat awkward gait, towards the street. Her head held high.

"Geoffrey, what are you doing out here?"

Slipping his coat back on, he turns and starts walking towards his sister. "I thought I could help someone, Margaret, but it seems I was wrong. It is late, what do you think, shall we retire?"

"Yes, I'm exhausted. I don't want to miss a minute of anything, however, we've been here for five hours now and I really desire to be home."

He offers Margaret an elbow, through which she hooks her white gloved hand, and they walk a short way down the road to where their bright red Brougham awaits. The driver, who has been pacing up and down to keep warm, is quick to step forward and open the carriage door.

"Milady," he says, holding the door wide.

Margaret nods her thanks, hitches up her skirts and steps inside. After a moment, when there is no sign of her brother, Margaret leans forward, sticking her head back outside.

"Are you coming, Geoffrey?"

Geoffrey is looking down the dimly lit street. He can't be sure, but he has a feeling the young redhead is watching them.

"Geoffrey?"

Pulled out of his sudden trance of intrigue Geoffrey moves, dipping his head he climbs in beside her.

Faith watches as the driver steps up onto his high box-seat and cracks his whip above the horse's heads. She doesn't like men, none of them. They are the bane of her life. Yet this tall, distinguished stranger had just crept under her skin and sparked her interest.

"Good night to you, kind sir," she whispers, before hurrying down the street. Needing to be up at six means that tomorrow is going to be a long day, and all because she let curiosity get the better of her.

Chapter 2

Sitting up with a start, Faith instantly knows she's overslept. Morning is being announced by the many noises stemming from the colliery. A high-pitched whistle interrupts the melodic chug-chug of mechanical arms, declaring the winding wheels and engine house open for business. Glancing over at her mother's empty bed she tuts, for she's been allowed to sleep in. Due to the lateness of the hour and the bitter cold of last night, Faith had crept under her bed covers fully dressed. She's glad of it now and shudders, as she thinks of dressing in a room where the air from her mouth drifts out in a flume of cloudy mist.

"Bertie, look, I'm a dragon." She blows into the air as she picks him up out of his little wooden cot. He throws his arms around her neck and nuzzles in close. "Oh my, how well I do love you," Faith sighs.

"You're going to be late." Her mother's voice booms up the stairs charged with irritation.

Grabbing clean clothes for Bertie, Faith hurries down the narrow staircase. Hearing the fire crackling, she's eager for its warmth. Standing Bertie in front of the hearth, she begins undressing him.

"Go on with you now, I'll do that. You get some food inside you before you go." Nell shoo-shoos her away with a flick of her hand and sits down in the only comfortable chair in the house.

"Want Faith do it," Bertie moans, sticking out his chin and pouting.

"I'll be home tonight to put you to bed." Faith smiles at him, and he stops his struggling against Nell.

"Promise?"

"I promise."

The one-up-one-down house is tiny, and being mid-terrace is protected from the elements somewhat, offering them a measure of comfort. It is home and that is all that matters. They sleep upstairs but spend the rest of the time in the living room, huddled around the fire, especially on cold days like today.

Sitting on a stool, Faith spreads a bit of lard over a chunk of bread and pours herself a glass of water.

"You were late last night," her mother scorns without a glance.

"I took myself to Ebenezer's."

Nell turns around in shock. "Never! What possessed you girl?"

"I was curious about all the fuss that's going on."

"Curiosity killed the cat they do say. So what do you think? Becoming a singing, smiling, worshiping fruitcake will you now?"

"Mam, don't be disrespecting them, I've never seen such respectful and caring people in my life. 'Tis loving and kind they appear to be."

"Well, if that's the case you ought to take yourself there more often. If some of it rubbed off on you I wouldn't be complaining." Nell's smile reveals her jesting.

"Mam!"

"Are you going to be working at the Miner's Arms all day?"

Faith swallows hard, dreading the news she's about to deliver.

"Mr Jones did lay off Bethan yesterday, and informed me that my services would only be needed in the morning to do the cleaning. Mr Jones and his wife will manage the rest of the day by themselves."

Nell rolls her head back and stares at the ceiling. Faith glances down at the table, biting her lip. *It's not my fault, Mam, it's not my fault.*

The eternity of fraught, drawn-out seconds causes Faith's spirits to plummet to her feet. Her eyes prick with unwelcome tears. As the bread-winner she will need to take on a second job, and quickly. Raising her chin with determined intent, she gets ready to declare she won't let them down. Before she speaks her mother turns and looks at her. The expected whiplash from a harsh spirit does not surface.

"Listen to me, Faith, nothing is ever as bad as it seems. You'll find another way to earn a living, be not disheartened. The Miner's Arms is not the only public house to be suffering since everyone has gone all religious. After your shift go you swiftly to every place possible and ask about work. Hear me good, do you?"

"Yes, Mam." Faith is bemused by her mother's soft tone, which of late has been brittle and blunt. "I won't let you down."

Nell turns her attention back to Bertie, giving no response, so Faith throws her shawl around her shoulders and heads out.

Brushing out the straw covered floor and wiping down the tables is completed far quicker than Faith would like; mostly due to the fact that with fewer customers there was less to be done. Mrs Jones keeps herself busy in the kitchen while Mr Jones, propping himself on a stool at the bar, reads the South Wales Echo, his white apron tied tightly around his middle. *Not too sure why he wears that apron, never gets either that or his hands dirty.*

"It says yer, that this revival is spreading throughout all the Welsh valleys. Would ew believe that, Faith? What is the world coming to when grown men would rather be singing in church late into the night than they would be having a sup or two of ale? The Pig and Pheasant has gone bust and the tobacconist on High Street has gone as well. The whole of Wales is going bonkers I tell ew, and that's the truth."

"Will you be closing down as well, do you think?" Faith's words fall hesitantly, her fear swirling in her chest as she crosses her fingers behind her back.

"I won't lie to ew, we're knocking on, but we've some money for a rainy day. No, our worry comes from not knowing how long this madness will last. Is it yer for good this time? The last one was mighty but ew know the people soon fell back into their old ways. Now it seems to me that no matter how fierce they bewail their religion, habits are more longstanding than faith. If this one passes too, we might weather the storm yet."

Faith recalls the fervor with which the people had praised God the night before, and couldn't imagine that such zeal would pass by in her lifetime. Keeping her opinion to herself, she purses her lips tight. She needs this job, few hours a day though it is, it will still help to pay the rent.

"Wouldn't you like me to stay and take care of serving once you open?" Her toes curl tight as she tries to squash the momentary flicker of hope.

"No, we had a total of eight lads in yesterday, and as much as I desire my house full once more and brimming to the doors with thirsty coal-blackened men, I've little expectation that it will happen today."

Masking disappointment, Faith puts her shawl on and heads towards the door. Just as her hand touches the handle she hears Mrs Jones approaching her husband.

"Did ew tell her she wasn't wanted anymore?"

Faith's stomach spasms as she takes a step through the doorway.

"Didn't have the heart. She's not like the other girls who work yer and ew know she is the only earner in her household. What would they do without our few shillings a week?"

"There's a fool you are, Mr Jones. Well I won't be so lily-livered. If things don't pick up next week then she'll have to go, and if ew don't pull your weight I might throw ew out too. Stubborn old mule, ew."

Faith closes the door discreetly. Her head is spinning, vision blurred and foggy. Outside she takes in deep gulps of air, trying to regain her composure. Bent at the waist, with her hands on her thighs she tries to still the waves of panic. Just then, she hears steps approaching on the cobbles. She hopes whoever it is will pass by without pausing, as she has no desire to talk pleasantries with anyone today.

"Fare you well?"

Recognizing the velvet rich tones as the toff from the previous evening, Faith groans inwardly. Unfurling her bent body, she stands up straight and looks up at him. *Oh, your eyes are as deep as the ocean, you pretty man. I'll wager all the women you meet chase after you, fluttering their eyelashes with artful seduction.*

Dragging her eyes away from his face she feigns disinterest. "I am well, thank you." She makes to walk away, but Geoffrey puts his hand on her arm. Shrinking back she glowers at him as if he's burnt her. He immediately withdraws his hand.

"I'm sorry if I've offended you. I merely wished to check that you're well." He takes a step back.

Faith is instantly mortified. *Since when have I lost my manners? The man is only trying to be helpful.* She tilts her head back to look at him. "Thank you for your concern, but truly I tell you, I am well."

His ocean-deep eyes full of concern reflect that he perceives her lie.

Please don't pursue. With hands clasped tightly together, Faith concentrates on the cobbles under her feet.

"My name is Geoffrey Driscoll, it is a pleasure to meet you, Miss…?"

Faith's head shoots up, her eyes widening in surprise. *Lord Driscoll?*

"Faith, Faith Miller." She dips a slight curtsy without thinking.

There's an awkward silence before Geoffrey gives a brief nod, as if making up his mind. "I've business at the bank, Miss Miller, so I will bid you farewell."

"Good morning, I hope your day is fruitful."

They walk in opposite directions. *Fruitful, I hope your day is fruitful? It's like Mam says, I'm a currant short of a fruitcake.* Having not gone very far, she's overcome with an urge to look back at him. She's gladdened more than a little when she finds him standing in the street staring at her. Not able to help the smile that flickers across her lips she turns and carries on walking, a sudden snippet of joy in her spirit. In her moment's happiness she forgets to guard her steps and her body rises and falls with a lilt to the right, clearly displaying the fact that she is lame.

"'Tis truly sorry I am for ew, Faith bach, *(dear)* but I don't need any more help. To tell ew the truth, Martha, well she started with me yesterday and you see I've known her since she was born. I'm sorry, lass."

There are a multitude of thoughts harboring sadness inside Faith right now. As if the day hadn't been bad enough, Mr Hughes has inadvertently just reminded her that she's still considered an outsider even though they'd lived in Abertillery for three years now.

"Have you tried the colliery? My cousin Mary, she started a couple months back she did. She's on the picking tables see, they don't earn that much like, still, it is something at least."

"I would rather dress as a man and go down the mines than starve. Alas, I've been there already, and they're not hiring, male or female."

"Ack-uh-vee! It will be with the closures going on, think there's hardly a public house left in all the valleys now. That, along with the fact this yer revival is healing people of many long term illnesses. Men be pouring back to work who've been laid up for some time now."

"Well, I wish that it would stop before me and mine should starve to death!"

The baker's face fills with compassionate understanding as he looks at her sadly. "Now don't be like that, the revival is the greatest gift that God could give us. The joy He brings us is beyond measure, and yet more than that. My niece has been going steadily blind for the last ten years. Well right as rain she is now, and she can see! 'Tis a miracle all right, and it's one that we're most grateful for."

For the second time that day, Faith is filled with remorse. "Forgive me, Mr Hughes. I've had a long day, and I'm weary to my bones."

"Yer, I have something for ew." The baker reaches behind and picks up two small loaves, which he wraps in brown paper. "I'm closing early as I want to get a good position in church tonight, so these will go to waste."

The lump in Faith's throat prevents her from thanking him, so she nods at him with water-filled eyes and hurries outside.

That's it then, I've been to every place possible and not one job going. So much for Abertillery being the booming colliery town we were advised to head to.

Her right foot is bleeding. She knows this without looking, for the wrappings are wet and yet no puddle has she walked through. In her tiredness she has been dragging her leg. Even the thought of her mother's rebuke doesn't give her the strength to pick it up. Although the pain's intense, if she could think of somewhere else to go looking for work, she would go in an instant. Her mother takes in the odd bit of sewing and can use the spinning wheel with grace and speed should anyone drop off a fleece or two. However, the local farms have started shipping their wool to industrial towns where they can spin the cotton at a cheaper rate. So it is rare indeed if someone knocks on their door these days.

From the moment Faith could walk, her mother had put splints on her leg, scolding her if she limped. 'Hide it well,' she had urged, 'or no one will offer you work, they will assume you are weak.'

Melancholy, her long-standing friend, nuzzles in close and whispers maliciously. *You useless cripple, what good are you to man or beast?* Faith's chin quivers as she tries to stop the anguish of lifelong pain from escaping. Her mood is now as gray and dull as the smog covered landscape, as she walks the long road through town. From this vantage point on the slopes of the hill she can see the spoil tip of the colliery and the collection of old, black cottages where they live, amongst the very poor.

'Slag-pile roughnecks' the town's folk call us, yet the only thing different between me and thee is a bob or two.

With her mother's well practiced, stern voice in her head, Faith tries her hardest to wall tall and straight, hoping to defeat the limp her body longs to succumb to. The late February wind is cold and cruel and no amount of hugging her shawl tightly can keep out the bitter chill. Her fingers are cold and her nose running as she trudges her way home.

Nell has been watching for her daughter through the small window, lit by a single candle. The moment she sees Faith stumble, she flies out of the door, running to wrap her arms around her daughter. For once, she is too upset to utter a rebuke at displaying her affliction in public.

Nell shuts the front door. "Help me with the bath," she says crossing the room and opening the back door. All Faith wants to do is sit on the chair in front of the fire, but she shuffles after Nell without complaining. They hoist the tin bath off the hook, where it hangs on the wall beside the back door. Taking one end each, they carry it into the living room and place it in front of the fire.

"Sit down, love."

Faith needs no second asking, and drops her frail body into the comfortable chair. Taking the kettle and the pan from the hearth, Nell carefully pours the water into the bath, and then refills them with water from the pump outside, before putting them back on the hooks over the fire. By the time they are boiling again, Faith has fallen asleep.

When her mother, stroking her head, wakes her a short time later, Faith feels disorientated. "The bath is ready. Into it you get, before it's cold."

"You had yours already?" Faith, with wobbly legs, stands up and begins undressing.

"Not dipped in yet, you go first today for you're as cold as ice. Here, let me do the bandages." Her mother kneels down and unwraps the blood-soaked cloths from Faith's foot.

She's surprised, for never once in all her twenty years has she been the first one into the bath, it was always Mam, then her, and Bertie last. "I haven't found a job, Mam."

"Aye, I thought not, or you would have come home earlier. Come on with you now, in you get."

"Where's Bertie?"

"Sleeping."

"Oh no, I promised to tuck him in."

"He waited for you. Worry you not though, for you can spend time with him on the morrow, when I go and see if I can find a job."

"Mam, I'm so sorry about everything."

"Hush-hush now." Nell begins washing Faith's long fiery hair, something she's not done since Faith was sixteen. The tenderness, which Faith has missed during the last four years, is almost too much to bear. Tears trickle down Faith's cheeks.

Nell wipes them away with her finger. "We'll get through this, like we always get through everything."

Bathed and dressed once more, Nell makes her daughter sit still in the chair and eat a potato she'd just pulled out of the fire, while she has a quick wash herself. Next comes the arduous task of emptying the bath, one heavy bucket at a time. Once that is done she fetches clean strips of cloth and comes to sit on a stool in front of Faith.

"Put it here," she says tapping her knee.

Faith lifts her right leg and puts her club foot on her mother's knee. Years of practice means that Nell has it dried and bandaged it in no time.

"You must've dragged it something awful," Nell says, wrapping the cloth carefully around the battered skin.

"I'm sorry, I tried to keep straight, it's just I got so tired."

"Hush you now, what's done is done."

"Do you think I'm cursed?"

"Tut-tut, silly child, of course you're not. It's just one of those things."

"Why *me*?"

Nell scrutinizes Faith's face as if counting the tiny pale freckles that run across her nose. "Why is it bothering you now? You've never questioned it before, you've always been so accepting."

Faith drops her gaze to her hands on her lap and feels her cheeks blushing. Curling her toes she hopes her mother can't read her thoughts about a certain lord.

A hint of a smile cheers Nell's face as she wraps her hand over her daughters. "Got yourself a beau, have you?"

Faith shakes her head sharply. "No, no time for that. It's just, well since I went into Ebenezer's, well… I can't stop thinking if God were real, why would He hate me so much."

"Oh, my sweet girl." Nell reaches over and encases Faith in a tight embrace as she tries to pour her love into her daughter. "If God were real, He surely wouldn't hate you, child, for yours is the most tender of hearts that anyone could own. What it is, 'tis just nature, I tell you. It does throw random acts of cruelty out into the world and thinks nothing of it. This wasn't done to punish you, it just happened, that's all. Come, let us retire and hope that on the morrow the sun does shine."

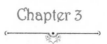

Chapter 3

March, although full of spring promise, still carries the bite of a cold north wind and the house feels colder than normal, on this gray Friday evening. The wood fire doesn't burn as long as coal. However, the wood kindling Faith gathered from the forest is all they have as their coal bunker in the garden has stood empty for weeks now.

The knock they were dreading comes. Three loud distinctive thumps on the wooden door announce that the rent collector is here. Nell uses her hands to smooth her hair, and then guardedly opens the door. Albert, or Mr Simmonds as he prefers, lifts his hat off his head an inch and comes inside without waiting to be asked. Sitting himself down at the table, he opens his hefty, leather-bound book, flicking through to the page he needs. Looking up he peers expectantly at the two ladies over his round spectacles.

Faith feels the need to support her mother and so goes to stand beside her. Both face the ruddy cheeked Albert, dreading what he will say when they tell him that for the second week in a row they haven't enough to pay the full rent.

Albert sighs, and it seems as if his chubby body deflates somewhat as he puts down his pencil. "How short are you, then?"

"Half," answers Nell, laying two shillings on the table.

He picks them up, counts them and then drops them inside his money bag. He notes the total against their name. After placing the money bag back inside his coat, he strokes his copious beard making a fine display of biding his time before speaking. At last, he seems to come to a conclusion and stands up, snapping his book shut, making both Nell and Faith jump.

"To be honest, like, I was talking to Mrs Simmons about ew I was, before setting off this evening."

"I do hope your wife is well, Mr Simmons," said Nell.

"She has never been better, praise the Lord. Her stomach complaints all disappeared one day in church at Christmas time and never came back; 'tis a miracle. Anyway, she did quote the Bible at me today when I mentioned you and she has shown me that we must be merciful."

Faith feels hope rise in her heart. Maybe they wouldn't be made homeless after all? She slips her hand into her mother's, and Nell gives it a gentle squeeze.

"So, before coming yer I did go to the church council and asked for their help like. They agreed, so they have. Since the revival, money has been pouring into the church coffers, and they're using it to send missionaries around the world, they are." Albert's obvious pride in his participation glows off him. "Well, I said to them like. If we are helping people far away, maybe we could also help someone a bit closer to home. So they said that, however short ew are for rent, and how short you might be over the next three weeks, they'll cover it for you. After that, they said, ew should be hard-working, and if ew are, then you'll be able to pay your own way!"

To Albert's shock and dismay, Nell throws herself at him and clings tightly to his stiff, portly body. "Thank you," she says, when he finally manages to push her off. "Please tell everyone at the church thank you, you are most gracious, and we will never forget it."

A bit uncomfortable at her affectionate display, Albert pulls at his coat to make sure it's straight. "Well, good-day to you, I wish you well, so I do."

"Good day, Mr Simmons," says Faith, grinning from ear to ear as she shuts the door.

The two women burst into laughter and holding hands do a jig around the small room.

"Me too, me too," yells Bertie, jumping up and down.

The initial joy of the reprieve begins to fade. They sit at the table looking at each other.

"That was the last of our money," says Nell with a weighty sigh.

"We should leave, with no end of the revival in sight there is nothing for us here."

"You're right. We've three weeks' grace to stay with a roof over our heads. Leaving just before rent day will put us at the end of April, when the weather will be kinder for traveling. We still need to eat, though, and my heart is breaking every time I pick up Bertie and feel his bones."

Later that night, as Faith sings songs to help Bertie fall asleep, tears form a river down her face, soaking the top of her dress. *I must do something - we are only here because of me.* Bending down she kisses the top of Bertie's forehead. *I swear that I will do everything I can to look after you.*

The faintest mellow light is creeping over the hills and Faith knows she has to be quick. Racing between the hedgerows, she keeps her skirts hitched high and her body bent almost double in an endeavor to stay below the height of the hedge. At last, she's on the edge of the Driscoll estate and skirting his arable land. Slowing down, she begins looking for a place where she can squeeze through the hedge. Finding a spot where the branches are thin enough, she's able to push herself through without too much effort. Using the gateways is out of the question, in case someone should come along the track and spot her. She crouches at the edge of the field for a moment, marveling at the beauty of the sun as it emerges over the hills, its magnanimous rays spilling across the deep green field. The land around town is blackened from coal-filled smoke and the lush colors surrounding her now bring joy to her spirit. Two crows caw to each other as they fly overhead, prompting Faith to move before the world fully awakes.

Practically lying down she reaches over and pulls a leek out of the dew-damp earth, staring at it for a moment with mixed emotions. Never before has she done anything dishonest, and for a moment she considers throwing it back. Then the memory of putting Bertie to bed crying because he was still hungry comes to her, and she stuffs the leek into her bag, immediately reaching over to pull another. Staying crouched and shuffling along the field she pulls leeks out from different areas, hoping the farmers won't notice gaps. A thrill of excitement rushes through her veins. She hadn't meant to get more than two, but ends up filling her bag and staying far too long. In her haste to be away before anyone arrives she forgets to stay bent as she rushes back down the path between the hedgerows.

The thumping of her heart feels painful as she walks through the outskirts of town making her way home, realizing she has left it far too late. Miners are already on their way to work. Many of them call out, wishing her a good day. Their constant chatter feels louder than the pit-head wheels clunking. With each acknowledgment they make towards her, her remorse grows. She wishes over and over that she wasn't carrying a bag full of stolen greens. They would lock her up if they knew what she'd done, and then their cheery greetings would turn to contempt. Suddenly, an image of the miners pulling her before the deacon of the church, forcing her to confess, comes to her. She shudders, she's heard all about hell and feels sure the fanatics would throw her there in a heartbeat if they knew how thoroughly wicked she is.

With utter relief she closes the door behind her and leans against it with a shuddering sigh, glad to be home. Just as she is standing up straight to move away, there come two sharp knocks on the door. Fear is instant. *Someone saw me!*

"Who's that at this hour in the morning?" Nell comes hurrying down the stairs wrapping her shawl around her. She pauses as she makes eye contact with her daughter, who's standing frozen in front of the door, clutching a bag. After a couple of seconds, there's another knock which throws both women into action. Faith races across the room and shoves the bag in the cupboard under the sink. Nell grabs the brush and starts attacking her wayward mop of auburn, gray-splattered hair.

"Coming," yells Nell, placing the brush down on the mantel, eyeing up Faith who is quickly washing mud off her hands in the sink. Nell puts her hand on the latch, but waits until Faith has finished drying her hands before opening the door. Receiving a jolt, she nearly stumbles on the step.

"Good day, madam."

"Good day," mumbles Nell.

Faith, curious to know who's thrown her mother into a tizzy, walks towards the door. *Aargh, calamities!* Taking a step backwards she tries to put herself out of sight of the dashing Lord Driscoll.

"May I come in?"

"Of course, yes, sorry. Please do come in, m'lord, although I must apologize for any disarray, *we've* only just risen."

Geoffrey removes his hat, ducking as he comes through the door, stepping over the threshold, but then remains standing in the doorway.

Faith, feeling her knees buckle, promptly sits down at the table. He appears so out of place in their tiny room that Faith feels bubbles of a giggle start and has to chew her lower lip to stop it. *He saw me! He must have, and now he's come to tell me he's going to the authorities.*

Faith finally gets her jitters under control. "Good morning, m'lord. I am sure you must be disorientated for there is no one here with whom you might wish to enter into a discussion,"

Geoffrey can't help it. The side of his lip quivers as he fights against a smile that wishes to display itself upon his otherwise completely stern looking features. "I can assure you that I am never in such a place that I don't know where I am, for indeed it is *you* that I wish to converse with."

Faith's heart skips a beat and the discomfort of it makes her scrunch her face in pain.

"Fare you well?" says Geoffrey taking a step forward.

Faith stiffens and stands up. "Well as anyone can be on this cold day when the wind is howling through the house. And you, sir, seem overly considerate with the health of a stranger. What is it that you wish to discuss?"

Geoffrey glances at Nell. "Is she always this forthright?"

Nell can't help a little snigger before snapping her mouth closed to quench it. "Well, indeed, m'lord, if you were to get a fair word out of her then it would be a day when the pigs would form an orderly line and wait their turn to be fed."

Now it was Geoffrey's turn to laugh.

"Come you on in now, sit yourself down by the fire and for sake of all that is righteous allow me to close the door before the neighbors do themselves an injury trying to listen to our conversation."

Faith stares at the cupboard under the sink. *Prison, and all for the sake of a handful of leeks!* Feeling his eyes burning into the back of her head, prickles run up and down her arms. She turns around slowly, and raises her chin in the air.

"Won't you sit yourself down in this chair, m'lord?" says Nell standing behind the biggest chair in the room.

Geoffrey does a slow sweep of the room, taking in the pots that hang from hooks on the ceiling over the table. There's a rickety dresser, a chipped brown earthenware sink, a spinning wheel plus a chair beside the open fireplace, which Nell has quickly reached down to stoke.

"We don't seem to have enough chairs, I shall stand. Please," he raises his hand towards the chairs, "you two should rest your feet."

Nell picks up the table chair and takes it to the fireside as Faith huffs before running up the tiny wooden staircase. Geoffrey, bursting with irritation, goes to the bottom of the stairs and calls after her.

"I shall not depart until we've had our deliberation, Miss Miller." Loud footsteps crossing overhead do nothing to disguise the exaggerated sigh that comes from the upper room, which irks him profusely. Her footfall on the stairs is heavy, and he decides to retreat to the hearth and wait for her there.

She reappears with a stool in hand which she promptly slams down on the floor between the other two chairs. With no further ado she plonks herself down, folding her hands sedately on her lap, while glowering at him questioningly.

The anger, of course, is simply masking her outright fear. *Does he know about the leeks? Has he come to have me arrested?*

"It won't take long," says Nell, nodding to the kettle that hangs over the fire. "I'll make us some tea. Do you drink tea, m'lord? The India and China Company recently opened a shop on the high street and I have to confess to being rather indulgent now and again. I just happen to have some in. Would you like some?" During her statement Nell has gone to the table, opened the tea caddy and popped some leaves into the teapot. She pauses in her chatter and looks at him, awaiting his response.

His eyes never leave Faith's face as he responds. "That would be most acceptable, Mrs Miller." There's a brief pause before he continues, "I wonder if you could enlighten me, Miss Miller."

"What about, m'lord?"

"It has recently come to my attention that there are people stealing crops from my fields."

Faith's mouth goes dry. Nell gives an involuntary yelp and slams the lid on the teapot to try to cover it up.

"If you know this, what is it that I could enlighten you about?"

"Pray tell me, what do you think would cause a person to do such a thing?"

He knows, he knows.

"Well, they might be hungry, mightn't they?" says Nell, lifting the kettle off the hook with a thick cloth.

Geoffrey can't take his eyes off Faith's pale face, which displays such rich brown eyes. Beauty such as he's never seen before, good gracious she stirs up something within him. "What do you think, Faith?"

Why does he play games? The man is cruel beyond measure. "There has been a certain amount of unemployment in the area recently. Maybe, if a family were to lose their income, they might seek other ways to feed their family?"

Geoffrey stares at her, understanding what she is telling him. His gut suddenly alights with angry fire against the injustice that is poverty.

Faith sees displeasure flash across his deep blue eyes, and shivers. Heat fills her belly as she looks him up and down. His silk and woolen suit and coat cost more than she could earn in a year and all of a sudden she despises him. "I'm not sure why you've come here today, but I want you to leave. My mother has just put into the teapot the very last tea we have, which she had been saving for her birthday as a treat and now it's gone. And for you of all people, who can drink the finest tea from sunup to sundown and never once consider the cost. So, m'lord, if that is all you wished to discuss, I would like to wish you farewell."

She stands up, bracing her shoulders and raising her chin. *I'll not play games with him; if he wishes to confront me then he should spit it out.*

Geoffrey also stands. His face, which had previously been soft, is now chiseled granite. God forgive him, for he didn't take insults well. "I'll get the grounds-keeper to employ more men to protect my land. I'll also tell him to inform anyone that if they're found stealing from my property there'll be no mercy for them."

It is a warning as clear as day. He knows what she has done, yet he is letting her off, just this once. Faith's sudden hatred of him lessens somewhat, but it is still there. "There was a time when any *decent* land owner would allow the gleaning of his fields by the poor."

"Faith!" Nell's shocked tone of rebuke knocks some anger out of her, and she lowers her eyes.

Geoffrey, insulted yet again, should be enraged, but all he can think about is the way her dark lashes fall and how salmon-pink and soft her lips look. "I've been led to believe that the revival has brought prosperity, that homes are enriched because men no longer waste their money in the taverns, on tobacco or gambling."

"Well, you may not have noticed, but there are no men in this home. And for your information, with the loss of customers taverns and inns are closing down all over Wales. When your way of living is that of a barmaid, well then, your home is certainly not in the overflowing flush of revival." Faith practically spits the words, she feels so bitter.

Geoffrey can't stand to see the pain and anger in her eyes and instantly wants, more than anything, to wrap his arms around her and take care of her. "I thank you for enlightening me, Miss Miller. I shall be sure to talk to the farm manager, and re-introduce gleaning until a time it is no longer needed."

"Do you *really* think that such a time will ever exist?"

"I certainly hope so." Whereupon, Geoffrey picks his hat up off the table, and heads towards the door. "Mrs Miller, it was a pleasure to make your acquaintance." With a brief nod at her, he opens the door and leaves.

There's silence for a moment as the two women stare at each other. "I take it that it's his leeks in the bag under the sink?"

Faith goes red and nods. Despite the reason she knows what she has done is wrong and despite her age, she still expects her mother to smack her legs with the wooden spoon.

"Leek and potato soup for supper then, that'll help put some flesh back on the boy."

Chapter 4

All Fools Day arrives promising a day of harmless shenanigans. It's been three weeks since the stealing of leeks, and in two days' time they plan to sneak out of the town under the light of the moon.

They've been cleaning until the tiny cottage is sparkling and smelling of vinegar, a task greatly impaired by the ever-present coal dust particles that hang in the air, marring everything they touch.

"They can say what they want about us, but they'll not say we were dirty," her mother had muttered again and again. The stone built privy at the bottom of their narrow garden was not left out. Nell had Faith cut up old newspapers into squares and hang them on the hook inside, much more than they would need over the next two days. A small act of rebellion against their outright poverty; no one would know they'd sneaked the old newspapers out of the tavern's bin.

Having been told about the numerous cloth mills in Gloucestershire that are turning their hand to tweed to stay in competition against the Scottish cloth flooding the market, Nell is convinced that is where they should go. It will take them at least a week to walk there, as they will have to carry their belongings and Bertie. Still, Nell is sure she will be able to find employment around the Stroud area.

Geoffrey, true to his word, had let it be known that gleaning was permitted once more, with the proviso that people should wait for the harvest to be taken in by his men first. Only then could they go and take what was left behind. He had given clear instructions that one foot of land around the edges of the fields was to be left untouched by the farmers. This meant that Faith, as well as others who are struggling, could carry home baskets full of vegetables.

In preparation for their journey they have wrapped potatoes in newspaper, along with leeks and cabbages, filling a box which they will carry between them. They are ready. Two more nights with a roof over their heads, and then they will set off on the next stage in their lives.

Faith is playing with Bertie, while Nell prepares the meal for that day, when a gentle knock-knock is heard. They glance at each other in sudden fright. Has someone guessed what they are planning? Faith stands up, lifting Bertie into her arms, as Nell goes to lift the latch off the door.

To their surprise it isn't the rent collector who stands there but a lady. Wrinkling her nose in concentration, Faith tries to recall where she has seen the woman before.

"Good day," says Nell, trying to mask the surprise on her face.

"Good day," replies the lady with eloquent decorum. "May I come in?"

Startled by her own lack of manners, Nell opens the door wide. "Please, do come in," she replies, flicking her head to the side and indicating the chair to Faith.

Faith puts Bertie down and quickly throws a clean rug over the chair. "Won't you sit down?"

The woman walks across the room, her eyes drinking in every aspect of the spotless, yet bare room. She sits down on the edge of the chair, her back straight as she removes her gloves with delicate precision.

Mother and daughter watch her, not knowing what to say.

Placing her gloves on her lap the lady looks up and smiles at Faith. "You must be Faith?"

Faith nods.

"I shall come straight to the point. I am in need of a new kitchen maid at the manor, and I've been informed that you are seeking employment. Is that correct?"

Faith nods again, this time with a giddy excitement bubbling inside her.

"The wage is two pounds a month. I will take you on a trial basis to see how you do." The lady's glance falls to Faith's right foot.

Not expecting visitors, she has forgotten to hide it under her skirts. The misshapen bandaged appendage is clearly on display. Faith pulls it back hurriedly so that her skirt covers it.

"Dependable as the next, I be. You can ask Mr Jones of the Miners Arms, he will tell you how hard-working I am." Faith clasps her hands tightly together and leans forward in an endeavor to impart how sincere she is.

The visitor smiles kindly, her crystal clear blue eyes sparkling with warmth.

Heaven's above, it's Lord Driscoll's sister. Did he send her here?

The lady stands and starts putting her gloves back on. For a moment both mother and daughter fear she has changed her mind.

"Mrs Lewis will expect you in the kitchen at six a.m. sharp. Make sure you are on time as she dislikes tardiness acutely."

"Oh, thank you, Lady Driscoll, thank you."

"Milady?" says Nell.

"Yes."

"I don't wish to appear ungrateful or crude, but the rent collector is coming on Friday, and we're short. We'll have to leave here if I don't have three more shillings for him."

"You need an advance on her wages before she even starts?"

31

"I will work harder than all your other staff, milady, I swear I will. I'll do extra hours as well," exclaims Faith quickly.

Lady Driscoll opens her small bag and takes out a purse, while she muses over the situation. *This is a miserable dwelling in a street fetid with poverty, in a mine-torn valley. These ladies might be amongst the poorest in town, yet they hold their character and keep an immaculate house.* At first, she hadn't agreed with Geoffrey's request but, having now met them, she understands why he wants to help. Having no qualms that the girl will indeed be most diligent to ensure her position, she passes some coins to Nell.

Normally a stern upright woman, Nell can't keep her emotions in check, and cries as she accepts the coins. "Thank you so much, milady. I'm so full of thanks, 'tis almost enough to get me to church to thank his nibs upstairs." She raises her eyebrows, glancing briefly at the ceiling.

"I will expect to see you at Ebenezer's on Sunday morning, then," replies Lady Driscoll walking towards the door.

Although Nell is slightly flabbergasted, in her eagerness to portray her thanks she nods profusely.

"Till Sunday then," she calls after her ladyship who has started off up the street.

"You're going to church!" yelps Faith as soon as Nell shuts the door.

"Well, didn't get much choice, now, did I? Can't go upsetting her ladyship before she's realized just how hard-working you are now, could I?"

"You've always been insistent that there's no such thing as God and those that go to church, well, they're just a bunch of babbling hypocrites!"

"I did indeed. This 'ere revival though, it changes people. You've seen it for yourself. All those men that used to drink away their earnings, well now they're giving their wages to their wives and their homes are more prosperous for it. It's not only that though, they talk different and you need to go a fair distance these days before you hear anyone cussing. Strange this revival is, Faith, and you know what? Now I've said I'm going, well I'm quite eager for it, I am."

A sudden knock on the door makes them look at each other in surprise.

Nell goes to open the door. "Never a caller except the rent man, and here we are with two knocks in one day."

Butterflies instantly fill Faith's stomach, with the desire that it should be Lord Driscoll calling upon them. She's disappointed when the door opens revealing a young girl.

"Mrs Miller?" the girl asks.

"That's right."

"What it is, see, Pa has sent me to ask ew if you will school me and my sisters in the art of sewing. He says he's fed up with us being a bunch of good-for-naughts, and wants us to be able to do something practical."

Nell laughs.

"Not going to lie to ew like, we ain't that bad. What it is see, we can do all sorts of things, but he don't consider things such as singing in the choir to be of worth, and is right poorly-bard *(fed-up)* of us being in chapel night and day. Says we've to help around the shop more and learn to be practical 'cos at the moment we is just like farts in a jam-jar, and he has nooo chance of marrying us off."

Both Nell and Faith are laughing. "I will be most happy to teach you to sew. You'll need to come here though, as there's my son to look after. When would you like to start?"

"I speak the truth, 'twould be best to please Pa, and for us to start tomorrow evening, if it's good for ew?"

"It is indeed. I'll see you tomorrow then, six o'clock?"

"We'll be yer," calls the girl, turning away.

"Wait, what's your name? And when you say 'we' how many are you?"

Looking backwards over her shoulder as she skips away she calls out, "Eva, and there are five of us."

"Five!"

Eva laughs and carries on skipping up the road.

"She's one of the butcher's daughters," confirms Faith, as Nell shuts the door. "I've seen his girls, they're quite flighty, but nice though."

"So, why doesn't their mother teach them?"

"She's dead, poor thing. I heard someone say she died giving birth to the youngest. I guess that's why the girls are a bit wild, having no mam to keep them in check."

"I'll go visit the butchers tomorrow and thank Mr Morgan for his custom." Mother and daughter lock eyes, both full of happiness at the sudden turn of events.

"Oh, let me hug you." Nell throws her arms around Faith.

"Hug, hug!" cries Bertie. Laughing they pick him up between them, including him in the merriest of embraces.

It is so dark when Faith sets off on the long trek to Driscoll Manor, even the morning bird call hasn't commenced. Nor does she pass any miners on their way to the colliery. In fact, the only other person she knows for sure is up is Mr Hughes, as the smell of bread wafting down the street makes her stomach rumble.

She's been walking down the lane towards the manor for some time before the birds' occasional chirps begin moving into full chorus. Fearing that dawn is fast approaching, which would mean she is late, Faith hitches up her skirts and begins to run as fast as she can. The further away from town she gets the more green there is to see. There is also a noticeable lack of industrial smell. Out of breath, hot and with a rapidly rising chest, she eventually arrives at the huge manor gates. Gazing in wonder at the stone lions perched upon the gate pillars she is momentarily struck with awe. At that precise moment, Lord Driscoll comes galloping down the path, having to pull his horse to a precarious halt to prevent running her down.

"What on earth?"

Shaking, and more than a little afraid at her near death experience, Faith steps to the side and onto the grass. "I beg your pardon, m'lord, I didn't think anyone would be on the path at this hour."

Stopping his horse from prancing, he leans forward and strokes the beast's neck. "Easy girl," he whispers. Straightening up again, he peers at Faith in the dim light of the setting moon. "What are you doing on the road at this hour, girl?"

Affronted at his tone, Faith bristles. "I am on my way to the kitchens to start my employ, m'lord." Her lips compress into a tight line, an unconscious demonstration of pure irritation.

"You've walked here?"

"Yes, m'lord."

"Good grief, you can't walk from home to here and back again each day. I shall tell Mrs Lewis to set you up in the servants' quarters."

"If it pleases you, m'lord, I prefer to remain at home and to walk here daily."

"You can't be serious?"

"I certainly am!"

"Duw Da!" *(Good God)* Irked beyond belief, Geoffrey is nevertheless surprised he has uttered a saying that rarely leaves his lips. This chit of a girl is impossible. Yet, he has an indescribable urge to take her in his arms. Without another word he nudges his horse and goes on his way, but distance isn't to dim the desire that is blossoming within him and his entire ride is dominated by the image of a beautiful girl with curly red hair.

Faith tuts as she stomps up the path towards the manor. *Who does he think he is?* Despite her brooding annoyance she finds herself thinking of the light in his eyes more than his words. *'Tis not right that a man should be so pretty!*

Moonlight still dances on the roof of the manor as Faith, turning a corner, at last comes into view of the impressive, gray stone building. In the center of the building protrudes the grand entrance way and receding inwards is a big black hole which holds an impressive ornate wooden door. Above the door a balcony encases a window with baroque masonry. To both sides of the door are four sets of paned stone mullioned windows. Sitting tall and stately upon the roof are four huge chimneys. Softening the harshness of the brickwork are clusters of bushes lining both the path and the steps to the entrance.

Proper grand. Nerves suddenly swoop in making her feel sick as she skirts the building looking for the servants' entrance.

With trepidation, she approaches what is clearly the kitchen door. Her steps are small as she clasps both arms around her body, trying to quell her nerves. Warm orange glows flood from the windows, and she can hear the banging of pots and pans as she lifts her hand and knocks gently on the blackened oak door.

Within seconds, the latch is lifted and the door abruptly opens. A young lady greets her with a broad infectious smile, causing Faith's tension to ease a little.

"Come ew on in now," a maid says, beckoning to her. Faith smiles her thanks and steps into the kitchen. Three young women, all dressed identically in charcoal dresses with full length white pinnies and wearing frilly white hair caps, are lined up behind a huge wooden table, doing various tasks. All of them look up smiling their welcome, and Faith heaves a sigh of relief. Having convinced herself they would think her scum, not worthy to be at the manor, it is reassuring to find they hold no such opinions.

"You must be Miss Miller."

Faith turns around to face the woman who has just entered the kitchen from the hallway. "Yes..." She falters, not knowing how to address the woman whom she assumes, by her attire, is the housekeeper.

"You may call me Mrs Lewis. Come with me." Mrs Lewis turns and leaves the way she has come in. Faith hastily follows after her. They enter a smaller room just down the corridor, which turns out to be Mrs Lewis' room. Faith will later learn that you never enter without being invited. The woman sits straight-backed in a chair on the far side of the table, as Faith takes a moment to absorb as much as she can. The spindly housekeeper wears a black skirt with a white blouse buttoned to the top of her neck. Several rows of lace fall from the neckline, layering her shoulders. Her gray hair is pulled back into a tight bun, and she wears her half-moon spectacles on the tip of her straight nose.

The room is full of cupboards and her desk stacked high with papers and letters. She appears both eternally busy and supremely efficient, if such descriptions can be given with a simple glance. Faith feels they surely could.

"Miss Driscoll informed me only yesterday that you were coming to us. There are rules within a household such as this. Most of them are never brought up, but they are there, lying under the surface of everything we do, making everything work like clockwork. There is a mutual respect between them and us, and a very clear definition of duties. I was quite shocked to be undermined by Miss Driscoll, and, I hasten to add, this is something she has never done before." Mrs Lewis taps her fingers on the desk, a clear indication of her annoyance at the situation. "Efficient though I am, I had no idea of your size, so we will fit you out the best we can. The last maid wasn't much bigger than you, but I think we shall be able to take the clothes in to fit you quite nicely."

"My mam is awfully good with the needle, Mrs Lewis. I am sure she could do it for me so that I am no bother to you."

Mrs Lewis pushes her spectacles up her nose and peers at Faith, the finger tapping having ceased. She hadn't been happy to be informed of new staff as she normally did all the interviewing and selecting of them herself. She had been ready to give the new maid a hard time until she was forced to leave. That way she could then select someone of her own choosing. After all, it is her job, and she is, and has always been, extremely accomplished in it.

"You're not Welsh then."

"No, Mrs Lewis, we came to Abertillery four years ago. 'Tis from Chester we come."

"I recollect Chester quite fondly. Beautiful walled city, but a bit too busy for me. I prefer the quiet of the Welsh hills and valleys to the rumble of industry. Still, my family hail from there so it is with warmth that I think of it."

A coldness, as deep as caves, cascades down Faith's back. Since they arrived four years ago, they have met no-one with ties to Chester. Her mouth goes dry, and she has a longing to sit down.

"Do you still have family in Chester?"

The question, although innocently asked, sends Faith into a panic. What if this woman was to make inquiries about them?

"No, Mrs Lewis, my father died of influenza some years back. When my mam could no longer keep the bakery going, we had to seek new employment. We were told that South Wales was booming due to the opening of more collieries, so we headed south, and here we are." The well-rehearsed twist on the truth falls easily from her lips.

The housekeeper surveys Faith for a short time, obviously digesting what she has just revealed. She grows uncomfortable. Will Mrs Lewis write to her relatives to ask them about a bakery which closed after the death of the baker? She isn't sure what the housekeeper thinks, but as soon as she starts talking, Faith sighs in relief.

"That must have been a great hardship? To lose both your father and your home and then set off to a strange place as well."

"Time is a good healer, they do say."

"They do indeed. I will tell you the truth. When Miss Driscoll informed me that you used to be a barmaid, I was expecting the worst of you. My encounter with such women has been to leave an impression upon me that they are the lowest of low; drunkards most of them. They certainly didn't have your manners."

Faith wants to defend the girls she worked with for they hadn't been that bad. Yes, they did like a drink bought for them by men with overly friendly intentions and wandering hands, and they did cuss as much as the men. But they had good hearts, each one of them. Still, she needs this job too much to risk upsetting the woman in front of her, so remains silent.

Mrs Lewis straightens, taking a deep breath. "I will show you to your room, which you will share with Olwen. You will have to tie your pinny around you tightly to disguise the size of the dress until your mother can alter it for you. Once you've changed, Esther will show you what to do. The girls take it in turns to rise early or stay late, and as this is your first day you may do a straight twelve-hour day. Tomorrow you can do the early with Olwen and follow her day. I take no nonsense from the staff so if you fraternize with the male staff you will be sacked. There are no second chances. If you are found stealing you will be handed over to the authorities immediately, and if you are slack in your duties you will be dismissed. Is that understood?"

Stealing? Has Lord Driscoll told her about the leeks? Faith feels sick, a lump appearing in her throat. She certainly doesn't want to be known as a thief.

"Yes, Mrs Lewis. However, about the room, I won't need one, thank you very much. I intend to go home at the end of each day."

"Pardon!" The shock on Mrs Lewis's face is, for a moment, quite comical. "Of course you will need a room, girl. The position requires you to work a twelve to fourteen hour day. You can't possibly put an hour's brisk walk either side of that. You'll be weary at the end of just a few days." The housekeeper pauses in her scolding and leaning forward, peers over the rim of her glasses to study Faith more closely. "Does your mother need looking after? Is that why you wish to go home?"

There is no way that Faith can reveal the truth about her desire to return home each day, nor can she lie and portray her mother in a bad light. "I have never been away from home on my own before."

Mrs Lewis sighs and sits back in her chair, relaxing. "How old are you?"

"Twenty."

"Don't you think that is a bit old to still be holding onto your mother's apron strings? I was under the impression that your mother needs you to have this position so that she can remain in the house?"

Faith drops her head in shame that people should know of their circumstances, but the shame of why she really wants to go home is even greater. There is no telling the truth. Not to this woman, anyway. She mumbles her reply, shame and guilt like blackened stocks holding her fast, refusing to release her. "Yes, Mrs Lewis."

The housekeeper stands up. "Come along and let's get you started."

"Mrs Lewis?"

"Yes?"

"I will need to go home, at least just for this night as my mam will be expecting me and I wouldn't wish her to worry. I will stay here after that."

"As you wish. Now come along, you have taken up far too much of my time as it is."

The day has been long and tiring. Faith is a little overwhelmed with how much she will be expected to accomplish each day. She will do it of course, for she is hard-working to a fault. As six o'clock approaches she's exhausted and realizes she's not looking forward to the long walk home at all.

Although she has tried hard not to think of Geoffrey, she has to admit that she is disappointed their paths hadn't crossed the entire day. Not that she could really expect them to, as she was in the kitchens for most of the time. She caught a quick glimpse of him before lunch when she spotted him having a discussion with Mrs Lewis in the hallway. As if aware of her gaze he had suddenly looked over at her, so she scurried quickly back down the hallway.

Crossing the yard, she heads towards a path leading off the estate, a different one to the one she had taken that morning. She had been informed that this was the one the servants used. Glancing at the sky she shivers, pulling her shawl tightly around her. It isn't raining but from the look of the sky a storm is heading their way and the wind is picking up. She will be lucky to get home before the deluge arrives.

"Hey, Faith."

Faith turns to see who is calling and spots Reuben standing near a cart, waving his cap at her. At lunch all the staff had shared a meal around the huge wooden table in the kitchen. There had been much chatter and a fair bit of laughter, most of which had been instigated by Reuben.

She lifts her arm in a half-wave. "I'm off home, Reuben. I'll see you tomorrow."

He runs across the cobbled yard. Stopping in front of her, he grins as he adjusts the cap on his head, pinning down his mop of golden curls.

"It's like this see. I'm heading into town m'self, on an errand for his nibs. Why not hitch yourself up beside me, Faith bach, and fetch a lift into town?"

Relief washes through her. "Will no one mind if I ride alongside you, Reuben?"

"Not a tiny drop. I be staying at mamgu's *(grandmother)* tonight, so I'll fetch ew back in the morning as well, see."

Faith bursts into a full-blown smile of joy. How wonderful has life been to them in the last two days!

Taking her hand, Reuben helps her step up onto the cart. He runs around the other side and climbs up. "Gee up, old girl." The huge brown Shire moves forward with a heavy clip-clop on the stone cobbles.

"I tell ew the truth, look proper grand sat there ew do, Miss Miller," and with the compliment Reuben winks.

Faith's head rolls back as she laughs with a gaiety she's not felt in many a year.

Watching them from behind the window is Geoffrey, who is relieved that the stubborn girl has accepted a ride into town. He's never met anyone before who both irritates and intrigues him the way she does. Somehow, the poverty-stricken, leek-stealing atheist has gotten under his skin and is dominating his thoughts.

Chapter 5

May has flown by and Faith is shocked at the speed of its disappearance, yet glad beyond measure for tomorrow is her first full day off. She is giddy with excitement about spending an entire day with Bertie and her mother. So far, she's only gone home on her half days off and the time always passes too quickly. Tonight, though, she will actually sleep in her own bed. Dreaming of holding Bertie the entire time fills her with happiness.

Faith has risen before the rest of the staff this morning to do as many chores as possible before they rise. She's lit the huge fire in the kitchen, stoked the ovens, scrubbed down the enormous wooden table and mopped the floors. Everything is spotless, ready for Cook to begin her day. If anything goes wrong today, and she can't finish her half day at the strike of two she will be without consoling. Today is Bertie's birthday, and she can't wait to show him the stone-cakes that Cook has helped her make for him.

She hears movement in the hallway so fetches the huge kettle off the rung over the fire and fills the massive teapot on the table. They are allowed two cups of tea a day from the general stores' cupboard, one in the morning and one with their evening meal. Knowing that Cook likes to start her day with a nice cup of tea, she has set everything ready.

"I tell you the truth I do, Faith bach, I have no idea what I did before you came."

Faith grins at her, knowing Cook has a soft spot for her and assuming it is her hard work and her eagerness to make everyone happy. Olwen is next in, rubbing her eyes as she shuffles towards the table.

"Ack-uh-vee, Faith! 'Tis wanting to put us to shame ew are with your early morning rises, if ew do it too much, Cook yer will be wanting us all up before the moon even begins its descent, ack-uh-vee!" *(exclamation of distaste)*

"Oh, now that has set me mind to thinking," smiles Cook. When she sees their alarmed faces, she's set off into a good old chuckle.

Two hours later, the early morning tasks come to an end. There's a bustle as the staff gather together in the kitchen for breakfast. Two flower-painted Staffordshire jugs filled with buttermilk take center stage on the table. A jar of bara lawr *(laverbread or cooked seaweed)* and a square of cheese sit in-between them with a huge loaf of freshly-baked bread placed at either end of the table. Fresh hot water has been poured into the pot so that a second, weaker, cup of tea can be had by those not wanting buttermilk. Or, in the case of the men, for those who usually want both.

There's a short silence as they take bread and cheese and fill mugs.

Reuben hasn't quite finished a mouthful of bread when he starts talking. "Not being funny like, but 'tis sure I am that Olwen is marrying Duw *(God)* and becoming a nun!"

"'Tis not too bright ew are and rubbish ew talk, garden boy," scoffs Olwen.

"Nooo, I tell you the truth see. I've seen ew sneaking into Driscoll chapel to pray at any moment ew get free. Sooo in love ew do look Olwen, does make me swoon with emotion!"

Olwen stands up and takes a swipe at him across the table.

"Enough!" barks Cook, although she's laughing.

"At the rate the Valleys is being taken up with this diwygiad *(reformation/revival)* then in all probability see, we'll all be sneaking into chapel. The Driscolls are thoroughly taken up with it I tell you. Lady Driscoll especially seems to be enamored with Duw. If she isn't visiting Ebenezer's then she's crouched over her Bible reading *most* enthusiastically." Everyone's looking at Mr Humphries, the estate steward, who while extremely efficient at his job, is normally slow to speak. Faith is sure this is the most she's ever heard the gentle giant say.

"You'll never find me in there," Faith blurts out.

"Nor I," says Reuben and the two of them share a smile of agreement.

"Never is a long time," says Fred.

Reuben, who is sitting next to Fred, nudges him with his shoulder. "And what would ew know of such things?" he teases.

"Well I tell ew the truth, see. I've been into church m'self on my days off, and wholeheartedly have I given my heart to Duw. This diwygiad has maketh me a changed man, so it has, most assuredly."

Olwen smiles, breaking off another chunk of bread while everyone else stares at the groom, waiting to hear more.

"Annwyl, annwyl! *(Dear-dear)* well machgen-i *(my boy)* hurry now, tell us what happened before we finish our fast," urges Cook, leaning forward over the table.

"Well it was me uncle, see. He did visit me from Bedlinog a short time ago. He told me how diwygiad had come to his tiny town, and he was so impassioned that he came to implore me to attend meetings at church. Well, I felt compelled to go, see."

"How did it come?" asks Esther with eyes like saucers.

Fred shoots Mr Humphries a questioning look, aware that they should be getting back to work soon.

"Take a moment, boyo."

"Well it's like this, see. It began with the headmaster, Mr Tomlinson. He heard that a young reformist called Evan Roberts was to preach in Dowlais. So after school one day he hitched a ride on the coal-miners' train and took himself off to the meeting he did. There, something happened to him, and he said he felt a presence in his being like that of fire. He caught the train home again, getting back to the village about quarter to ten. As he got off and started walking down the street he was so filled with Duw that he couldn't go home.

"He was in his best silk tails, wore a fine silk hat and carried a cane with a silver knob ending. I tell you the truth, he was in his finest. Yet there, in the cobbled street he did fall to his knees."

Esther gasps, putting her hands over her mouth.

"Mr Tomlinson began to sing hymns right there and then. At that moment my aunt Mary and her neighbor Mrs Morris was walking home when they heard this singing. So they hurried themselves off to the caretaker's house see, and knocked sharply upon the door. Mrs Burns, they did declare when the door opened, you've locked the vicar in the church!"

Cook snorts and the others chuckle, even Mr Humphries smiles.

"Never! Mrs Burns answered them, to which they both declared, oh yes indeed, we can hear him singing! So Mrs Burns grabbed the keys, and they went rushing over to the church but, as you can imagine, there was no one inside. Mrs Burns did complain like, saying she should have known better, for the vicar did have a weak voice for hymns. Yet they could all hear the singing, coming from nowhere but coming from everywhere. They started walking up the steep street, and they heard a man call out - the headmaster's gone crazy, he's on his knees yer singing! So the women rushed on, finding men pouring out of the tavern with their ale glasses still in hand, and men from the billiards room coming out still with cues in their hands. All of them gathering around Mr Tomlinson."

"I should imagine that was a proper-daft sight," chips in Olwen.

"Well, Mr Tomlinson by this stage had tears freely flowing down his cheeks as he sang about the blood of Christ. Everyone was muttering, 'Mr Tomlinson's going mad,' but then the strangest thing happened. One of the men from the tavern, still with beer glass in hand, got down on his knees beside the headmaster see, and started singing."

"Well I never!" exclaims Cook.

"One by one…" Fred pauses for dramatic effect, nodding slowly and looking each of them in the eye in turn. "They all went on their knees, every last one of them, including my auntie, her neighbor and Mrs Burns. Before long they were all weeping and praising Duw, and not a preacher amongst them! I tell ew the truth, Bedlinog has not been the same since. The whole village, every last one of them swept up in diwygiad!"

"I think the time of breaking fast is long gone." Everyone pushes their chairs back and hurriedly makes themselves busy tidying away the things from the table, as Mrs Lewis walks through the kitchen. "I would count the storage room with you, Mrs Jones."

"Certainly, Mrs Lewis," replies Cook with a curt nod.

Fred makes a hasty retreat towards the door, as the housekeeper starts walking towards the pantry. "Young man."

He freezes, fearing a rebuke for taking so much time in his story telling. "Yes, Mrs Lewis?"

"It pleases me that you are a man of religion, would to God that every man were. But talking of diwygiad I believe is an error I do not wish you to repeat on this estate. A godly man's faith is long-standing and righteous. What are these revivals except an excuse for people to throw decorum to the wind and to wail and shake in church. None of which I believe glorifies God but only edifies themselves, that is why revivals do not stand the test of time. We will not discuss this again, do I make myself clear?"

"Yes, Mrs Lewis." Before she has a chance to say anymore, Fred hastens out of the door. If the housekeeper opened the door, she would hear him muttering as he heads towards the stables, "If it's good enough for his nibs and her ladyship, well then, 'tis good enough for me!"

For the last two hours, Faith has been at the grueling job of polishing the silver cutlery and heaves an exaggerated sigh of relief as she places the last spoon back in the case. Peering at the strapping mahogany fusee-dial clock on the wall, she registers that there is only half an hour to go. Shutting the case gently, she carries it into Mrs Lewis's room. No one is there, so she places it on the desk and hurries back to the kitchen.

"What would you like me to do now?"

"Go and get ew washed and dressed, Faith bach. I know Reuben will be waiting to fetch ew to town so go on now, get ready."

Faith doesn't need a second prompting. Picking up a jug of water that stands next to the huge porcelain sink, she races upstairs to the small attic room she shares with Olwen. Washed and changed in no time she feels giddy with excitement. Back in the kitchen everyone else has settled into their afternoon chores.

"Yer, see I have found a tin for ew to take your bake-stones *(Welsh-cakes)* home in. For a treat, Faith bach, sprinkle them with sugar before you put them in the tin."

Faith runs across the room and hugs her. "Thank you, are you sure the mistress won't mind?"

"Eee, I've not time for a cwtch *(hug)* be off with ew now."

49

Faith pops a kiss on Cook's plump, rosy cheek before picking up the Huntley and Palmer's green and red biscuit tin. After sprinkling a tiny bit of sugar over the top, she places the bake-stones carefully in the tin, which Cook had peppered with a little flour.

"Do you think Reuben will be ready?" asks Faith to the room in general. Just then the door opens and Reuben himself comes in, all a fluster.

"Talk of the devil!" says Cook.

"Ack-uh-vee Faith, I tell ew the truth, 'tis mighty upset I am that taking ew into town I cannot!"

"What's happened? Are you all right?" asks Faith rushing to his side.

"Oh, I be fine in it, but 'tis master Driscoll, he has set me on a task in the herb gardens which means I won't be finished until dusk. 'Tis right sorry I am, lass."

"It's not your fault, don't fret. I am happy to walk, the sun is shining and it is a beautiful day."

"But, but…" Reuben's looking at where her feet would be if she wore her skirts a little higher.

Faith can't help but bristle. She had been mercilessly teased and tormented by other children when she was young and had grown up with a fierce determination to not only prevent people from seeing her club foot, but also from letting it affect the way people saw her as a whole.

"I've managed twenty-one years of walking… all by myself, today will just be another one." Irritated, she turns back to the side where she put her shawl and tin. Too warm to wear it, she throws the shawl over her arm and picks up the tin.

"Goodbye, everyone, I will see you tomorrow eventide."

"Hwyl fawr," *(goodbye)* echoes around the room.

"I'll step out with ew for a bit," says Reuben opening the door for her.

They walk across the cobbled yard in silence and as they reach the gate to the servants' path Faith stops and looks up at the strapping young man.

"I can go by myself from here, Reuben. You get you back to work now."

Reuben wipes his hands on his shirt and puts his hand in his pocket and pulls out a scrunched up handkerchief. He offers it to her. "I know how fond you are of your brother, see. So I did buy these for him, on my last visit to town."

Faith takes it from him and opens it with intrigue.

"'Tis clean like, I kept the cloth safe."

Opening it up, Faith discovers six pieces of peppermint creams and smiles up at his sun-kissed face. "Thank you, that was very thoughtful of you, Bertie is going to be delighted."

Reuben blushes and in that moment, she realizes he is sweet on her. She's taken aback that anyone should like her in that way and the smile slides off her face.

Seeing shadows swoop down on her expression causes Reuben concern. Reaching out, he touches her arm. "Ew all right?"

Shaking herself, she answers quickly, "Yes. Yes, I am fine, but I best be off now."

Watching, Faith sees a little sadness fall into his eyes. Not wanting to cause anyone hurt, she doesn't stop to think but throws her spare arm around him and gives him half a hug. The grin springs back on his face as he tips his cap at her before spinning on his heels and heading off to the kitchen gardens.

It is by chance that Geoffrey decides to get up from his desk and stretch at that moment and is by his study window in time to see the friendly embrace. His body, especially his face, is abruptly awash with heat. An irksome annoyance boils in his belly as he watches Faith set off down the path. He knows the household rule of allowing no fraternizing amongst the staff, for Driscoll Manor is an honorable estate. He would have Reuben dismissed.

Rapidly following that most irrational thought comes logical reasoning. Firstly, it had quite obviously been an embrace between friends, not lovers. Secondly, what reason does he have for over reacting in such a way?

He looks up at the wall to portraits of his mother and father that hang side by side. Both had died before their time and yet their life, though too short, had been full of love and laughter. Lord Michael Driscoll had often been cause for gossip in the House of Lords, where he would frequently bring up the opinion of his wife to his peers. Geoffrey himself isn't fond of visiting London, especially the House of Lords. If it wasn't for the fact that Margaret remains as yet unmarried, he might consider throwing respectability to the wind and leave it all behind for good. He enjoys managing the estate and the peace and quiet of home. Yet, he still feels he has a voice to be heard so takes every opportunity to stand up for the commoners. Maybe, once Margaret is suitably married to a man of position, he can then afford to be a little selfish and remain at Driscoll more.

His own marriage, or more accurately... the lack of, is often the talk of high society. Driscoll is a moderate estate, not having the wealth of many of the other Lords, but it is a name long-standing in society and due much respect. Many a mother has ushered her daughter under his nose on social occasions, hoping that her fair charms might win him over. He can honestly say he's not met a single woman whom he'd even consider spending his life with. Not overly worried, he has passed the need for marriage and the further need of an heir over to God and is well rested in the assurance that He will see to delivering the right woman to his side.

He's returned recently after spending just over a month in London, and in these last few days he has found himself constantly looking to catch a glimpse of a beautiful redhead who always remains in his thoughts. That his first sight of her should be of her embracing another man brings him huge discomfort.

Chapter 6

Repetition makes days blur into each other, causing time to sweep through the Valleys without a care. Like the perpetual winds that whip the sea, making it sway in an eternal waltz, so time quick-steps merrily and carefree before it is gone in a blink of the eye.

The last day of June! Faith can hardly believe it and yet here she is, in Mrs Lewis's office receiving her second wage. The stern housekeeper has grown on Faith and a fondness for the skinny, black and white clad woman has wormed its way into Faith's heart.

"What will you do with yourself this afternoon, will you go home?"

"No. Not today, Mrs Lewis. Mam has persuaded Mr Morgan to visit church with her and his girls, and after that they're going on a picnic away from town and the smog."

"And you don't wish to join them on the picnic?"

"His girls are lovely, but so much chatter comes out of them it doesn't half give me a pain in my head. I was thinking of going for a walk and taking a bite to eat with me."

"I can understand that. Enjoy your solitude."

"Thank you." Faith rushes out of the office and up the stairs to get changed out of her uniform. She will miss seeing Bertie, but she is tired so for once will relish a piece of time all to herself.

Having stripped and quickly washed, Faith considers her small choice of clothes, wondering what a walk in the countryside might warrant. The tiny lanes will be dry, as it hasn't rained for several days. However, it might still be muddy in patches, so she decides on a dark brown skirt and a blouse. Her wardrobe consists of two day-blouses and one for Sunday-best, which as yet remains unworn since her mother only gave it to her last month. Although she isn't going out where dressing with decorum is required, she has a desire to feel pretty, so picks up the white laced blouse her mother made. Pulling it on, she tucks it into her skirt and then can't help hugging herself. She doesn't know where Nell got the delicately soft cotton and lace from, but Faith thinks she will swoon, as she feels so richly thankful for the lovely item. Quite frankly, she has never owned anything so pretty in her entire life.

The other thing her mother did for her on her last day off was to take her to the cobbler who made a soft shoe for her right foot. He had been extremely kind and worked very hard to try to make it look like the boot she always wore on her left foot. It didn't really look the same but in comparison to the dressings her mother used to tie around it, it was amazing. Faith is delighted every time she puts it on. Her misshapen foot bends inwards at an awkward angle, and is always being scraped along the ground. For the first time in her life, Faith walks without fear of making it bleed. Life is good and she feels full of joy.

"There's tidy ew look, Faith bach. Pretty that blouse is," says Cook.

"Mam made it for me," replies Faith beaming.

"I've made ew a little something to eat," says Cook, nodding at the table.

Faith goes over and picks up a small parcel wrapped in brown paper and tied with a piece of string. "Thank you."

"Ew enjoy your walk like, but mark my words and be sure to be back before dark, for I tell ew the truth, poorly-bard I'll be if ew's not back by then."

Faith rises on her tiptoes and kisses Cook on the cheek.

"Go on away with ew," says Cook going back to rolling out pastry.

Geoffrey is talking with Fred when he catches sight of Faith making her way down the path. He brings his discussions to a close and walks into the yard to watch her. He hates knowing that she walks the long distance into Abertillery to see her family and if etiquette would only allow it, he would run after her and offer her a ride in his carriage. Reaching the fork in the path she turns right, instead of left which leads into town. Both curious and concerned, for there is nothing but hills and forests to the right, he marches into the kitchen.

Before he gives himself time to think of the impression he's going to make, he blurts out to Mrs Jones, "Cook! Where has the girl gone to? She's headed right, towards the hills?"

Without portraying her surprise at his question, she carries on lining plates with pastry ready for her rhubarb pies. "Well, m'lord, she is on her half day off so ew needn't worry that she's skiving, see. 'Tis not like that is our Faith, good lass she is, sir."

"That's not what I meant, I only inquire because... well you don't think she will lose herself out there do you? You know, Mr Humphries did inform me only the other day that gypsies are passing through the valleys."

"Sir," she says wiping flour off her hands on her apron, "that is most kind of ew to be concerned, but worry ew not. She did promise me to be back before dark."

Geoffrey stands there wavering in his opinions as to what he should do next. He's very aware that both Esther and Olwen are staring at him with open mouths and that his questions will be frowned upon and considered most peculiar.

"Very well," he says, as a lack of anything else has come to him. Nodding at Mrs Jones, he marches through the kitchens, heading towards the hallway. "I look forward to your pie. Rhubarb is my favorite."

Cook's beaming as he leaves. For years, he's been telling her that rhubarb is his favorite pie. Although he knows she knows that, he can't help himself confirming the fact to her, ensuring they never ceased to be served.

"I'm not going to lie to ew girls, I've been cooking for him since he was knee-high and I know his stomach better than he knows it himself and that's the truth!"

Olwen and Esther giggle as they carry on scrubbing pots.

"Why do you think he asked after Faith?" asks Olwen.

"Now that, I don't rightly know. Sincere I am in saying, that eggs have no business dancing with stones." She is met with two blank stares.

Sheer pleasure radiates from Faith's spirit as she drinks in the beauty of the Welsh hills. Such peace descends on her, like nothing she has known before, and she wishes she could capture it in her hands and hold it close forever.

Leaving the industrial part of the Ebbw Fach valley, with all its noise, stinks and dirt, Faith heads as far eastward as she can. Every step takes her further away from the touch of black that she has gotten used to over the last few years.

Here the hills are fresh, displaying their beauty with unassuming benevolence. Splayed languorously, they generously invite all to partake in their wondrous greens of ups and downs. Today, Faith drinks in their beauty as one parched of tranquility. It is only as the bliss of silence envelops her that she realizes that the noise of the collieries is suffocating. The never ending clanging of metal upon metal, of men shouting orders and metal gates slamming is mixed with the steam pistons, the shift-bell ringing and the chuff-chuff of the steam trains as they carry away the black-gold.

She finds a clearing where the hill levels out a bit and gives up a flat piece of land for her to sit on. Spreading her rug on the grass she sits down with a sigh. Despite her joy and her new shoe, her foot is hurting and it feels good to rest it. Unwrapping the paper parcel she discovers chunky bread pieces, slices of roast beef and a boiled egg still in its shell. She taps the egg and starts peeling it whilst drinking in the view of the valley below. After her meal she lies back on the rug and watches the sky, as fluffy white clouds bob along their way. *This must be like heaven, if heaven were real.*

Comfortable after her food, Faith drifts off to sleep after pulling into her thoughts the rather handsome face and sparkling eyes of Geoffrey.

"Faith?"

Faith wakes with a start and screams when she sees a face right in front of her.

"Faith, it's only me, I am sorry to have alarmed you. It's beginning to get late and I thought maybe we should head back before it gets dark."

Faith sits upright and takes in the soft orange glow that radiates over the hill tops, realizing that in fact the sun is already well on its way down, and there isn't much chance of getting back to the manor before dark. She rubs her eyes before scrutinizing Geoffrey's face.

"How did you find me?"

"Actually, I wasn't looking for you. I fancied a walk and was enjoying it. Then I spotted you asleep and decided to sit and wait for you to wake up, to make sure nothing happened to you. I didn't want to wake you, but it is going to be dark soon, and I really do think we should head back."

Faith scrambles up and brushes down her hair to make sure it isn't astray, and then her skirts. She's very self-conscious over the fact that Lord Driscoll had been watching her sleeping.

Geoffrey stands up. "You look just fine." He smiles, picking the edge of her lace frill that lies over her shoulder and pulling it so it lies straight below her neckline again. A flush, deep and hot, sweeps over her face as she gazes into his deep blue eyes. It's an inappropriate touch which sends thrills racing through her body, making her tremble.

"Are you cold?" He's concerned, he hasn't worn a coat and so has nothing to wrap around her. He bends down and picks up the rug. As one in a daze Faith allows him to wrap it around her shoulders. His fingers briefly skim her neck as he puts it around her. Tingles race across her skin and she catches her breath. She's never felt more alive.

What's happening to me? "We'd best head back, but I think you should go on ahead as I won't be able to keep pace with you."

"Nonsense, I can't leave you on your own, it will be dark soon. Besides, I think I would quite enjoy some company." His smile is endearing, wrinkles at the corner of his eyes holding her captive.

She doesn't know how old he is, but he's obviously several years older than her, yet that doesn't seem to matter. Faith is tall for a girl, but he towers above her, forcing her to look upwards. She has only ever seen him in his immaculate suits before, but today he has come walking wearing casual trousers and an open shirt. The look suits him, making him look younger and more approachable, and she is gripped with an urge to reach up and run her fingers through his light brown hair. Shaking her head, she tries releasing herself out of the moment's magic.

"Shall we, then?" she says as she starts walking.

At first, they walk without speaking; both lost in their own thoughts about the person they walk beside.

At last Geoffrey breaks the silence. "Tell me about yourself."

"There's not much to tell."

"Of course there is, tell me how you found yourself in Wales, for a start."

Oh no. Loathing to lie, Faith repeats what she has told the housekeeper, keeping things as short and as close to the truth as possible.

"I'm sorry about your father."

"I'm lucky, I still have my mam." She glances at him sideways. Questioning the other staff about him, she had found out both his parents had died within a short time of each other a few years back.

"Yes, that indeed is a blessing, and you have a brother too. It's good to have family. I don't know where I would be without Margaret, she is a huge support to me and runs Driscoll exceedingly well. I will miss her when she goes."

"She's leaving?"

"She will one day, when at long last she finds someone worthy to marry."

"Oh."

"Most women her age have been married for several years already, but she is waiting."

"What for?"

"For someone, she says, who will be her best friend forever and someone who loves God just as much, if not more, than she does."

"Is that possible?"

Geoffrey looks down at her, one eyebrow raised.

"Oh, I didn't mean any insults by that, I just meant that she loves God an awful lot I've heard, and I wondered if it was possible for anyone to love Him more than that, that's all."

Geoffrey laughs softly and Faith is drawn to the sound, as thirst to water.

"She does indeed love God *an awful lot* but just take a look around Wales and you will see she is not alone in that matter. Have you never gone back to Ebenezer's since that day we met?"

"No, my mam's going now though, and I've noticed she's changing. She's always smiling and singing, I've never seen her so happy. Whether it's from going to church, or the fact that Bernard now goes with her, I don't know."

"Bernard?"

"The butcher. Mam's been teaching his daughters in womanly duties. He's trying his hardest to marry them off, you see."

Geoffrey chuckles. "Is he indeed, and how many daughters does he have?"

"Five."

"Five? Good Lord, no wonder he is trying to marry them off, a household full of girls must be, well… trying, I should imagine."

"And what if you have daughters and a household full of women, what will you do then? Marry them off from the crib?"

"I must first find a wife before I can have daughters. In all honesty, I would consider myself extremely blessed if I had five daughters."

A wash of relief floods Faith, although she has to shake herself to recognize that his desire for children is of no concern to her.

"And what of you, Faith, do you wish to have a gaggle of children?"

Ice-like cold drops down her back, leaving her unable to answer.

"I'm sorry, that was probably too personal a question of me to ask. I understand that most women wish to be mothers but that there are also a few that do not have that desire within them. It is none of my business if you do or do not."

Suddenly, Faith's daydreams explode into a million splinters of desire, causing her pain. "I have always wanted a large family. I would love a family with lots of children and grandchildren running around the house, filling it with joy and love."

"You say that so sadly."

Faith's step falters, and she stops as pain ripples through her again. "To have children you must first have a husband."

"Well, that will be easy for you, Faith. You are beautiful, and any man would be lucky to win your hand."

Stop, stop, stop. Tears come despite the order not to, and Faith starts walking again in the hope that Geoffrey won't notice.

"Faith?" Geoffrey places a hand on her arm, forcing her to stop. Tears are falling, and reaching up he wipes them away. "Why are you crying? Do you think no one will have you? Is it because you're lame? You mustn't think that. Do you know I don't even notice your limp anymore? All I see is you, beautiful you."

The tears ease as she studies him, more than a little awed at the fact that he keeps calling her beautiful, as she's always considered herself extremely plain.

The light drops as the sun slides behind the hills, whilst the two of them search for the soul behind each other's eyes. A silent acknowledgment transpires between them, as without words, they realize there's something in the other they want to know better.

"They'll send out a search party if we don't return soon." The spell's broken, so they step back from each other.

Geoffrey knows she's right, but he also understands that she has just deliberately put a stop to whatever was transpiring between them. He doesn't understand why, and in his bones he feels that there is something she is hiding. Right then and there he determines that he will find out her secret, so he can ease the pain of it. He will have to, for he has also decided that Faith Miller is the woman he wants to grow old with.

Chapter 7

He has to admit she's stubborn. As he diligently seeks to bring them into contact, she continues sidestepping him in every encounter. If she had been a lady of high society he might have thought her coy and become annoyed, but he knows her well enough to perceive she isn't playing games. She is simply avoiding him, not trying to lure him into a deeper relationship.

He accepts her mute challenge and spends many an hour devising ways in which he can win her heart and trust.

Unbeknown to him, he is causing Faith great distress as hiding from his attentions becomes ever harder. She will not let history repeat itself and for the love of her mother and Bertie she will make him see that she cannot be brought around. After the last four years of shame and grief she has finally come to a place where her mother can be proud of her. They are in a time of blessing, she knows it well, and will do everything in her power to keep it like this. Having the Driscoll lord pursue her with no regard to what the other servants think of her is killing her inside. Her appetite wanes and day by day she grows thinner. Mrs Jones does her best to plump her up again, but Faith can't be persuaded to eat anymore. Everyone watches on, worrying about her but not knowing what to do.

The other servants have gone to their beds and Cook and Faith are alone in the kitchen.

"Will ew stay a while with me, lass?"

Faith, always eager to please, puts her apron back on. "What needs doing?"

Cook taps the side of her large chair. "A cwtch is what I need, Faith bach. Come ew yer and sit with me." Faith approaches with hesitant steps. "Tidy ma, cariad." *(Come here, love)*

As soon as Faith sits on the arm of the chair, Cook lifts up her arms and gives her the tightest of hugs. Immediately, Faith begins crying, unable to stop, the sniffles soon become great racking sobs.

"There, there." Cook gently taps her back. "Let it out."

As the leaking of sorrow-filled water starts to subside, Faith's shuddering eases off.

Cook strokes her hair as Faith gives the occasional deep sigh and catches her breath. "Not being funny like, but if ew don't tell me everything right now I'll be proper poorly-bard, so I will."

For the next hour Faith pours out her story to the compassionate Mrs Jones, who listens without interruption as Faith pours out a torrent of past pain.

"I was sixteen when I met Harrison. He was so handsome with his golden locks and laughing eyes. When he started courting me I couldn't believe my luck. How could the son of a lord, and one so striking in his features, be interested in me? We lived in a bakery at the time. My father was really a gifted baker. He made wonderful fancy things for the gentry so we were always busy. At first, he was right proud that a lord's son should show an interest in me, for he believed being a cripple meant no one would want me."

"Now why would ew think that?"

"Because he told me, and told me often. I always wanted to learn how to bake, but he told me I was no good for anything more than cleaning. He'd always wanted a son so being a girl I was a disappointment to him. Being a cripple made it worse, he told me more than once he wished he had drowned me at birth."

Cook gasps. "What did your mother say?"

"I never told her, I didn't want to put my pain onto her. She always worked so hard and took such good care of me. I knew there was nothing she wouldn't do to help me."

"Well, seems they was like chalk and cheese then, your parents."

"They were."

"So what happened with this yer dandy then?"

"At first he would bring me flowers and ask me to walk with him. He was so charming and kind, often bringing me gifts."

"Would he now, indeed! Was your mother not wary of him?"

"Harrison asked me to keep our courting a secret until we were sure we were in love."

Cook tuts. "Ew should never keep secrets from your mother."

"I know, but I didn't know that back then. Pa had seen Harrison come into the shop for me but for some reason he never told Mam. I thought Harrison loved me, I was sure he was going to ask me to marry him."

"Oh lass, so you gave yourself to him?"

"Yes."

"Oh, you poor thing." Cook reaches in her pocket and brings out a handkerchief and blows her nose loudly.

"The deed only happened once. Afterwards, he left me lying on the grass and just walked away. I was so shocked I just lay there and cried. I tried to forget him but within a couple of months it was obvious that I was with child. My pa beat me with a belt and called me the most dreadful names. Mam fought him off in the end and got belted herself for doing so. The next day after he found out he dragged me to the mansion where Harrison lived. I was so ashamed. Up the front steps he made us go, yelling to see the lord. We were ushered into the library and a very long time later Harrison and his father came in. Harrison denied even knowing me and when his father asked him if he was sure he replied laughing, saying he would never go near a disfigured ugly cripple like me."

Faith sobs as the painful memory surfaces again.

Cook blows her nose and wipes her eyes. "What happened then, Faith bach?"

"Harrison's father offered my pa quite a large sum of money to go away and to keep our lies to ourselves. I couldn't believe it when Pa took the money."

"Oh love, I'm right sorry ew had to go through that. Did ew lose the child then, before its time?"

Faith shakes her head.

"It died during birth?"

Faith shakes her head again.

Cook sits up straight, cupping Faith's chin to make her look up. "So what happened to the child?"

Gritting her teeth, Faith tries to hold back the tears which refuse to stop. "Bertie," she finally admits, as tears flow like a river.

Cook sits back in her chair, clearly shocked. "Bertie's your son?"

"You mustn't tell anyone, promise? Please, Mam couldn't bear the shame if everyone knew we'd been lying about him. Please promise me."

"Hush, child. Of course I'll stay quiet. My lips are sealed tight, 'tis not my secret to tell. Ack-uh-vee, but it's such a sad tale. So tell me, where is your Pa now? And why have ew come from Chester to us?"

"After the disgrace, the gentry stopped visiting the shop. Each day Pa grew more and more hateful towards me and Mam, and often got drunk and took to beating us. The more my bump showed the worse he got. Then one day we woke up and he had gone, packed a bag, took all the savings and walked out on us. Oh, Cook! It's all my fault that Mam had such two-fold shame brought down on her." Faith breaks down into another bout of painful crying.

Cook holds her tightly, waiting for the crying to abate once more. "What happened then?"

"The landlord came a few days later and demanded the rent, saying Pa hadn't paid him in months and that he wanted all the money. When we told him we didn't have it, he sent in men to take all our furniture. My mam's parents had been quite wealthy, you see, and had passed down to my mam beautiful antiques that were her pride and joy. In one day we lost everything."

"That must have been very hard for her."

"She told me they were only possessions and that the most important thing was that we had each other. She made inquiries and was told that the coal mines and steel works in South Wales meant there was always work to be found, so we left Chester and began the walk here."

"Ew walked the whole way being pregnant!"

"No, we often hitched rides with farmers and the walk was broken up with stays in various villages. Mam had a plan that kept us moving from place to place, until Bertie was born. Once he arrived, Mam told me from that moment forward he was her son and I was never to breathe a word about what had happened to anyone. She said it would be hard enough to find myself a husband being lame, without having a child as well. So we arrived in Abertillery and have lived a lie ever since."

"Your mother is a very special person, understand that don't ew? She has done her utmost to protect ew."

"I know, and I've done nothing but bring shame into her life. Now Geoffrey is determined to know me and I think I might die from it."

"He's not done anything inappropriate, has he?"

"Oh no, he's a perfect gentleman, he seems only to want to talk to me and to get to know me. But he must desist, he simply must."

"I must admit to being bemused by his advances towards ew, but I know he's an honorable man. Have ew thought that maybe his intentions might be leading to marriage?"

"I have day dreamed that very thing. But it can never be because a husband would have to know everything about me, and I have promised Mam that no one will know about Bertie. Besides, in what world does a Christian lord fall in love with a non-believing maid?"

"There's naught as queer as folk and stranger things have happened. As to finding out about Bertie, well, I do think ew do Lord Driscoll a disservice by thinking about him in such a dim light."

Faith untangles herself from Cook's arms. "I can't take a chance. He must never know about Bertie. I need to find a way to make him stop seeking me out."

"He's off to London tomorrow, so ew'll not see him for a month. Maybe by the time he returns he will have forgotten about ew."

Faith misses the twinkle in Cook's eyes. *Oh, I hope not!* "You're right, and I am probably making a mountain out of a molehill. Thank you for listening to me, I do feel better now."

"That's grand, a problem shared…"

"Is a problem halved. Nos da *(goodnight)*." Faith gives her one last hug.

"Nos da bach, and don't let the bed bugs bite."

"Nor you."

"Faith?"

Faith stops in the doorway, turning back to look at Mrs Jones.

"What happened to your father? Do ew know?"

"We heard he gambled all the money away, and one day, when he lost and had no coppers to pay over, that men did beat him to death."

"Oh, that's dreadful."

Faith doesn't answer as she's not so sure it is dreadful, but she nods as if agreeing, and then takes herself off to bed.

As Faith makes her way up the stairs with a heavy heart, she is unaware that Mrs Lewis is standing in her study doorway watching her.

"Ta da!" Faith cries as she throws open the door.

"Faith, Faith." Bertie comes charging across the room and throws himself around her legs. Putting down her bag, she picks him up. He immediately snuggles into her neck. "I missed you, Faith."

"Not half as much as I missed you," she says showering his head with kisses. "Hello, Mam."

"Hello love, 'tis good to see you."

After shutting the door, Faith puts Bertie down, and then joins Nell, who is sitting at the table shelling peas. Popping a kiss on the top of her mother's head, she smiles. "You're looking good, Mam."

70

Nell puts the peas down and gets up. "The kettle's hot, I'll make some tea." There's a hint of a smile on her face, causing Faith to wonder what's causing it.

With the teapot brewing they sit and exchange general information for a short time, until Faith can take it no longer.

"What's happening? I feel like there's something you're wanting to tell me."

Nell fills two small teacups then, as she puts the cosy over the teapot, she looks at Faith and nods. "There is indeed some news to impart."

"Well?"

"Where to start... well, I'll tell you in the order that they happened."

Faith smiles, she's curious to know why her mother for once seems a little tongue-tied.

"Two Sundays back I was sitting in Ebenezer's. Bernard now, he's paying for a family pew he is, oh 'tis so much better than standing at the back of church. You get to see everything going on. The wooden pews, well they're not that comfy when you get to sit there for four hours in a row, but still, 'tis much better to sit than stand."

"Mam?"

"I know, get on with the telling. Well we were all sat there like, and everyone around us they were all praying out loud. Most had their arms in the air and all were crying out their separate prayers. Mrs Davis, well she cried out in one place, 'Lord I know the pub isn't a respectable place for you to go into, but please would you go in there and fetch my brother, Henry out so that he might know you.' Lots of people were sobbing and thanking the Lord for showing His mercy on them. Then all-of-a-sudden I was taken with urgency, so I poke Mrs Tanner – who's in the row in front of us, in the back. When she turns around, I do say to her, 'for Heaven's sake Mrs Tanner, tell me what I must do to be saved!' Right then and there I repeated the prayer asking Jesus to come into my life, and for God to forgive me of my past sins." Nell, overcome with emotion, clasps her hands over her face and starts weeping.

"Oh, Mam." Faith jumps up and comes around the table to wrap her arms around her mother.

"I'm sorry that I stopped showing you love after you got with child, Faith. I didn't mean to hurt you, and I do love you, but God has shown me that I used lack of affection to punish you, and I am sorry to the bottom of my heart, so, so sorry."

"Oh, Mam, I'm sorry too, for bringing such shame down on you." They hold tightly to each other, and weep on each other's shoulders. It's only when they become aware that Bertie is now sobbing in the corner that they stop.

"Hush little one, we are crying happy tears, there is nothing to worry about," says Faith picking him up and bringing him back to the table. She keeps him on her lap, wiping his tears away. Comforted, he lies against her chest and wraps his tiny arms around her.

Mother and daughter look at each other across the table, both aware that an invisible barrier between them has been lifted.

"Well, to carry on, seeing me converted had an immediate effect upon Bernard, so he pokes Mr Tanner in the back and says the same thing I did." Nell laughs, "I have discovered that the Lord is good, Faith, good indeed. He has blessed me greatly, I see that now. Not only has He given me you and Bertie, but now... Bernard has asked for my hand in marriage!"

"Oh, Mam, that's wonderful."

The sparkle in Nell's eyes fades a little as she looks at Faith with a more solemn reflection. "It is wonderful, indeed. However, once we are wed I shall be moving into the butchers."

"That's good, isn't it? No more rent worries?"

"The thing is, there is space for me and Bertie, but with five daughters there isn't a place to set up a bed for you." Nell chokes on the words.

Faith reaches over and grabs her hand. "'Tis all right, Mam. I have a very comfortable bed at the Driscolls. This is good, it really is."

"Bernard says that as soon as one of his daughters gets married then you will be welcome to live there too. Until then, there is always space around the table for days when you visit."

"That's fine, really. Please stop fretting, this is wonderful news."

Nell searches her daughter's face for any hidden hurt, and finding none she relaxes and smiles.

Faith takes a sip of her tea. "What have you told him about Bertie?"

Nell, who was just about to drink her tea, puts her cup back down without taking a sip. "Nothing, he knows Bertie is my son, so what is there to tell?"

Scrutinizing her mother's face, Faith's heartbeat quickens and her palms begin to sweat. "You didn't tell him the truth?"

"There's nothing to tell."

"But is it right for you, a new Christian, to be lying to your betrothed?"

"He hasn't asked me if Bertie is my son and I have not spoken otherwise, so I haven't lied."

"I think your silence is deception."

Nell sucks in her breath. "Bertie is *my* son. I have raised and loved him. With Bernard, he will have a father. He'll grow up to be a butcher and will never want for anything again in his life. Would you take that away from him?"

Faith swallows; the lump in her throat is painful. "No," she whispers.

That night Faith pulls Bertie into her bed and holds him tight. As he sleeps in her arms, tears cascade unchecked, soaking her sleeping-dress.

Chapter 8

August is hot and humid, making work almost unbearable. However, an air of tangible excitement grips the day as Miss Driscoll had announced yesterday that she's arranged for them all to go to the seaside for the day.

"What it is see, is that if we cool off for the day then we'll be able to work harder on Monday morning."

Olwen throws a cloth at Reuben. "Naught between your ears ew have."

"Miss Driscoll is away for two days now traveling with the Evan Roberts crowd, so that is why it is easy to grant us all such a privilege."

Everyone turns to look at the housekeeper.

"Will ew be coming along with us then, Mrs Lewis?" asks Cook.

"Indeed I will. I have a sister who lives in Newport, so when you are at Scarog Bay, I will be visiting her."

"So we'll all be going then?" says Reuben, smiling at Faith's back as she finishes washing dishes in the sink.

Faith stops what she's doing, and wiping her hands on her apron turns around to deliver the news she knows will receive a measure of opposition. "I won't be going. I shall take the time to visit Mam and Bertie. She's getting married in October and I wish to spend time at home before things change."

The expected protests fly out from everyone almost at once, but she remains calmly resolved.

A short time later, the staff board the wagon carrying picnic baskets and overflowing bags. Reuben's the driver, but before climbing up he comes over to Faith, who has come outside to wave them off.

"Ew sure ew won't come with us?" His eyes plead with her.

"I'm quite resolved, Reuben, go on with you now and enjoy your day off. Olwen is mighty pleased to be spending time with you."

Reuben runs his hands through his thick locks, looking at Faith, puzzled. "Why do ew push me away? Ew know I only have eyes for ew, and since the day ew arrived. I would court ew Faith, if ew would allow?"

Faith steps back. "You best get going, they're waiting." Right on cue, the rest of the staff start yelling at Reuben to get his arse up onto the wagon.

Faith waves as the jolly day-trippers head off to the beach. Esther, taking off her straw sun-hat waves it at Faith, until turning a corner they go out of sight.

Locking the kitchen door with the big iron key Cook had given her, Faith sighs and turns to make her trip to town. Although she has a hot walk in front of her, she is happy to be outdoors and not sweating over the huge kitchen ovens.

Having walked about half-way she's just approaching a fork in the road when the cycle club come charging down the lane. Smiling, she steps onto the grass verge, allowing them to pass. The gentleman riders from all walks of life call out to her, raising their caps as they ride past. Towards the end comes little Robert, and as he sees her he pulls over and stops.

"Not going into town to see your mam, are ew?"

"Yes, I am, is something wrong?" Alarm quickens Faith's pulse.

"No, no, 'tis nothing wrong. It's just they've gone away to Cardiff for the weekend with the butcher see. He's shut up shop an' all. Just don't want ew walking that far 'tis all, if you're only after seeing yer mam."

"I was. Thank you for telling me, you've really saved my legs from wasted exhaustion."

He wipes his sweating brow with the back of his arm. "Welcome, Faith, 'tis welcome ew are." Pushing off, he races after the other cyclists.

Disappointed beyond measure that she has missed a trip to the seaside, Faith turns around and starts back towards the manor. Having not gone far, she hears a carriage behind her. She steps close to the hedgerow, allowing the vehicle to pass by on the narrow lane. It has only just passed her by when it stops, the door opens, and Geoffrey gets out.

There's a whoosh in her ears as her blood seems to drain out and then floods back in with rapid speed. He has been in London longer than expected. No-one had been sure why or when he would return. Faith had begun to imagine that he'd found someone new to be interested in, and although this is what she wanted she couldn't help being overcome with jealousy.

For a moment they stare at each other, lost in their thoughts, until the driver gives a gentle cough.

"Faith, come on, I will take you back to Driscoll."

She shakes her head.

"Don't be silly. The sun hasn't even risen to its height yet but already the day is sweltering. Get in." The last part has been an instruction that brooks no argument.

Rushing forward, Faith accepts the offered hand and climbs inside.

"You've been into town early, or were you at home last night and just now returning?"

"I was on the way to visit my family but was informed they have gone away for the weekend, so I am returning. You should know, m'lord, that everyone has gone to the seaside for the day, instructions from the mistress. I will be able to serve you, though, and fetch you something to eat. Will cold meats and salads be acceptable? I mean, I can light the ovens, but they take a long time to heat."

Geoffrey stares at her as she clasps her hands in her lap and fidgets with her skirt.

"I've missed you, Faith."

Turning her head, she looks at him from under her fringe. He'd spoken so softly and with a measure of sadness. Searching his face, she longs to know what he's thinking.

"Have you missed me?" he asks.

Sometimes, there is a need to lie. "I've been working hard. I've had little time for idle contemplations."

The rest of the ride is made in silence. Arriving at Driscoll, Geoffrey helps her out and then pays the driver, who despite the rising heat is still clad in his black tails and top hat. While he is doing that, Faith takes herself off around the back of the house to the kitchen entrance. She has just unlocked the door and is stepping inside when Geoffrey appears behind her. She's sensitively aware of his closeness and longs to lean into him. Acutely alert to the fact that they are in the house alone, she hurries to put the table between them.

"Can I get you anything, m'lord?"

"Actually, I would love some tea, if that's not too much trouble?"

"No, of course not, I'll make it straight away. Would you like me to bring it to the study for you?"

Geoffrey pulls out a chair and sits down at the table. "No, I will have it here."

Faith blushes. *What's he doing?*

The tea is made in awkward silence, the only interruption being when she places a cup before him and he tells her to fetch another.

She places the cosy over the teapot to wait for it to brew, then stands with her hands behind her back, not knowing what to do next.

"Please sit down."

She pulls out a chair and sits down.

"Is there nothing pleasing about me to you?"

Going a deep crimson Faith stares at the table.

"I am saddened by your lack of interest in getting to know me. I consider myself a kindly person. I have title and lands and I'm told by quite a few that I am rather fair of face. Is there nothing in me which appeals to you?" Faith remains silent, head bent. "Is it my age? I know thirty must seem awfully old to you, but I can assure you there are many marriages that work extremely well. Even when the husband is considerably older and the gap in years much greater than ours."

Faith lifts the cosy, places the strainer over the cup and pours out the tea.

"Do you have nothing to say to me?"

"'M'lord, I am so thankful that you spoke to your sister about me and that I came to work at Driscoll. I love my job here, and my mam and Bertie have never been so comfortable. I am also beyond expressing how grateful I am that you told no one about the leeks."

Geoffrey raises one eyebrow at her, smiling. For a moment, Faith teeters, and has to hold fast to her resolve.

"But you must understand, I have no desire to ever be married *nor* to have a beau. I am happy with the life I have."

"From my limited experience with women, I find they are prone to changing their minds."

"I will never let you court me."

"Never is a long time. Pray tell me, why am I so abhorrent to you?"

Faith is disconcerted. "You're not. No, indeed, you certainly *aren't* that. I agree wholeheartedly with those who say you are fair of face. Do take my breath away sometimes, you do."

Geoffrey laughs and leans back in the chair, tension visibly slipping off his shoulders, for he's just been given hope.

"Then what is it, Faith? Will you not court me until I declare my love for you?" Internal conflict flashes across her face, and Geoffrey is once again convinced that something holds her back. "I believe with God, that all things are possible. Whatever it is that afflicts you so, I wish you would trust me so that I might pray on your behalf and beseech the Lord to bring you peace."

"Please stop."

Geoffrey rubs his thumb over his lips, wondering what to do next. "I promise not to talk romance with you, if you will spend the day with me and get to know me. Come on, Faith. I'm seriously not a bad person, you know."

Faith looks at him, her brown eyes big and round as her mind swings with indecision. *Out of the fire and into the frying pan.* "What would you like to do?"

Geoffrey's grin lights up his eyes. Faith can't help smiling back. "Have you ever ridden a bike?"

"No?"

"Then it shall be my pleasure to teach you. Give me a moment to change, I'll be back soon." Just as he's about to enter the hall he turns back to look at her. "Don't go anywhere, will you?"

Amused, she shakes her head.

Like a schoolboy he charges up the stairs two at a time.

He returns a short time later, his trousers held tight around his ankles with clips, and wearing a soft white shirt he hasn't bothered tucking in.

"Here," he says, handing Faith an item of clothing. She stands up, holding it out in front of her. It looks like a skirt but it is actually sewn in two parts like a pair of trousers. "They're Margaret's, I don't believe she has worn them in years so she won't mind if I give them to you."

Faith blushes again. "I am not so sure she won't mind."

"I promise you it will be fine. Go and try them on."

Smiling as she heads up to her room, she's excited to be trying on something so modern. Surprisingly they fit well, although a little loose and definitely a little short, but it means Faith can swing her legs around and still be covered up. She looks down at her right foot which is now clearly on display. Her instinct is to put her skirt back on, to hide her disfigurement from him. *Then again, it might just be repulsive enough to put him off me.*

Entering the kitchen again she finds Geoffrey is not there. The door's propped open, so she goes out into the yard. He's just coming out of the storage shed pushing a bike. When he sees her, a boyish smirk appears on his face. She grins back at him as he pushes the bike over, never once looking down at her feet, although they're clear to see.

"I've lowered the seat, try it for size."

Nervous now, Faith steps over the bar and positions herself on the seat. Once sitting down, she can only reach the ground with her toes. She tilts the bike slightly so her left foot is fully on the ground supporting the bike, and her right foot clangs against the chain. She looks up at Geoffrey in dismay.

"Here." Kneeling, he picks up her right foot.

Shaking her leg, she makes Geoffrey let go. Her heartbeat drums loudly in her ears and she feels sick. No one but Nell has ever touched her foot, not even Bertie. Loathing for her deformity seethes through her mind every day.

"I'm sorry, I should have told you what I was going to do. I'm just going to place it on the pedal, that's all."

He reaches for her foot again and Faith has to fight every nerve in her body to resist pulling away from his touch again. Astonishment makes her look at him with new eyes.

"Right, now you're ready. I'm going to hold onto the handlebars so you don't have to worry about falling and you are going to put your other foot on the pedal, right?"

Nodding, she cautiously lifts her leg. The bike instantly wobbles and she puts it back down again straight away.

"I won't let you fall, I promise, surely a little wobble doesn't scare you?"

"Oh, but it does!"

This time, Faith trusts his strong arms to hold the bike securely, putting her foot on the pedal despite the wobbling. The next quarter of an hour is spent with Geoffrey running alongside the bike as Faith gets to grips with the pedals and keeping her balance. Eventually, he let the bike go and she goes riding down the lane by herself, laughing giddily. Stopping first proves a little difficult, but she soon gets to grips with leaning to the left so she can put her good foot down to steady herself.

Her first fall has Geoffrey turning white, which sends Faith into fits of giggles. When she's confident enough they decide to go for a ride down the lane heading for the stream on the far side of the estate. Geoffrey fetches a canteen which he fills with water and Faith throws together cold meats, cheese and bread, placing the lunch in the basket, which hangs on her handlebars.

The feel of the breeze against her cheeks seems to wash away all her cares, making her laugh and filling her with joy. After an hour of riding they find a place to stop. Working together, they spread the rug under the shade of an old oak. Then, after dividing the food, they sit in comfortable silence as they eat, watching the birds sing and dance in the air over the water.

With the picnic's finished, Geoffrey lies back, placing his hands behind his head and closing his eyes. Faith lies down on her side, propping her head up, using her arm as support.

"Thank you for today. Riding a bike is so exhilarating and I would never have experienced that without you."

Geoffrey rolls onto his side, propping his head up, mirroring her position. "I can honestly say it has been my utmost pleasure." As he gazes into her doe-like eyes, he wants to say so much more but, conscious of his promise, he remains silent and doesn't reveal his feelings.

After a short rest they take a walk and Geoffrey regales her with stories from his childhood, making her laugh. He loves it when she smiles; her whole face changes, sparkling with life. And when she scrunches up her little Grecian nose in laughter, he yearns to reach over and kiss it. He knows, as the day proceeds and they get to know each other better, that he has found the woman he wants to spend the rest of his life with. A need to make her smile and laugh is now deeply embedded in his heart.

Riding the bikes back in the late afternoon proves to be difficult for Faith, as the path slopes gently upwards and she's tired, so her right foot keeps slipping off the pedal. In the end they walk side by side, pushing the bikes.

Back in the courtyard Geoffrey takes the bike off her.

"I'll make some tea and bring it to the dining room for you, m'lord."

He'd just been so happy and now he feels as if she's thrown a bucket of cold water over him. He is so hurt he can't answer so walks off without replying.

Faith is lighting the stove to boil some water when he comes into the kitchen.

"I will be in the library. You can bring my supper there." His voice is cold and emotionless as he walks into the hall without a backward glance.

Chapter 9

Merry laughter fills the tiny house as they sew the finishing touches into their dresses for the wedding. The giddy sisters have embraced not only Nell into their family, but also Bertie and Faith. Their generous spirit of loving kindness is something that Faith had not expected.

Eva already considers Bertie her little brother and sole responsibility, dedicating every spare moment to playing with him. They are in the yard now as she chases him around with a jug of water, threatening to soak him. The back door's propped open, allowing the musky-mellow September breeze to wash through the house. As the women sit with dresses on their laps, they stop to watch, laughing at Bertie's 'please catch me' run.

"I've finished!" declares Maisy standing up and holding her dress against her body.

"'Tis beautiful, the soft blues reflect your loveliness so well," says Nell.

"Well enough for Douglas to notice me, do ew think?"

Everyone agrees it will surely catch the young man's eye.

"And what if you get his attention but then after a while he returns home to Scotland?" asks Faith.

The glaze pales in Maisy's eyes. "I tell ew the truth see. That very same thought has been in my mind most repeatedly. Do ew think a man might take to a new home, if he was to fall in love?"

"I am sure he might, but before you fill your head with questions of love you should take the time to get to know him, find out if he's worth his salt," answers Nell. "There, I'm finished now as well."

Ooh's echo around the room as the girls gather around Nell, who's holding up her deep-blue dress for all to see.

"Oh Mam, 'tis right pretty."

Nell smiles at Faith, joy radiating from her eyes.

"The pearl buttons Lady Driscoll gave ew just add that special touch, don't ew think Mrs Miller?" says Elaine, reaching up to touch the row of tiny buttons that run down the back of the dress.

"Lady Driscoll gave you buttons?" asks Faith in surprise.

"Yes, but more than that, she asked me two Sundays after you started working at Driscoll, if I would have use of some odd sewing things she had. Of course I said yes. The next day she turns up with a huge hamper of bits and pieces, including the fabric which I used to make your new blouse. All sorts of pretty trinkets inside, which I have been putting to good use."

"She's sooo kind," sighs Amy.

"Yes, a more respectable lady there never was," says Nell.

Faith cringes, had her mother just compared her to lady Driscoll and inadvertently reminded Faith of her failings?

"Shall we go now?" asks Maisy. "I'm sure Pa will be waiting on his swper *(supper)* now."

"Yes, let's go," replies Nell. Before they go, she takes the dress upstairs, and lays it carefully upon Faith's bed.

With chattering louder than the chug-chug of the colliery winding-engines' pistons, the ladies pile into the butchers. Suddenly, Faith is overcome with a feeling of not belonging. She turns to Nell. "I'll be off now."

"Don't be silly, come along in and have swper with us," says Amy, linking her arm through Faith's.

"Stay, Faith, stay," adds Bertie, before running into the house calling out Eva's name.

As she watches him it feels as if her heart is breaking; he's already comfortable enough to think of the butchers as his second home. She's glad he's happy, and over-the-moon that he will never be hungry again, but a bitter, bitter taste fills her mouth as she realizes he's moving away from their special bond.

Nell puts her arm through Faith's other arm, and so she's marched into the butchers by the two women who won't let her leave. The wonderful smell of lamb cawl *(stew)* floats through the house and shop and pulls everyone straight to the kitchen.

"I'll not lie to ew. If ew hadn't turned up soon see, into that pot I would have dived and not sure I be, that there would be any left for ew women," says Bernard, his smile making wrinkles appear around his eyes.

His daughters leave him gazing lovingly towards Nell, as they flurry around fetching bowls, spoons and cups to the table.

"I hope ew don't mind, but to dinner I have invited old Griffin." Bernard looks at Nell with raised bushy eyebrows.

"Of course not, the more the merrier I say," answers Nell.

"I'll fetch another stool," adds Amy.

Just as the last pieces of the evening meal have been put down on the table, there's a knock on the back door. Amy pulls open the door and lets the old miner in.

"Boy, do ew have good timing, henwr! *(old man)*. Sit ew down now at the head of the table, Griffin."

"Well, it's like this see. If ew get invited to dinner where the house is tipping over with the weight of sooo many women, well, ew have to take no risks see, and get yourself a plate of swper before it's all gone."

"Ach-y-fi, 'tis rubbish ew do talk henwr," laughs Maisy. "Now pass me your bowl and let me fill it before I change my mind."

Everyone's bowl is full, and chattering comes to a stop as all eyes turn to Bernard. "Let us pray," he says. They bow their heads and he thanks God for the food they are about to eat, and for *lots* of other things as well. At one point his daughters begin opening their eyes to look at their newly converted father, wondering if he would come to an end so they might eat their cawl before it goes cold. "Amen," he finishes.

"Amen," is repeated by all, including Bertie. All, that is, except Faith.

Munching on a large mouthful of bread, Bertie looks at Faith. "Ew didn't say rr'men."

Faith's face flushes rich pink as she reaches for some bread and ignores him.

"You didn't say rr'men," Bertie repeats.

"Not everyone prays, bachgen *(lad)*," says Bernard.

Faith looks at him in gratitude.

"Why not?" asks Bertie.

"I'll tell you later," says Nell. "Now eat your food."

Bertie stares into his bowl, clearly puzzled and frustrated.

"I don't believe in Him, that's why I don't talk to Him," Faith blurts out.

The sisters carry on eating and passing things around the table, whilst Nell, Bernard and Griffin openly stare at her.

"What? Would you have me lie to my own…"

"Faith!" Nell half rises from her chair as she realizes what her daughter is about to say. Both women glare at each other, but when Faith doesn't finish the sentence, Nell slowly sits back down.

"Ew know, those penstif *(obstinate)* pit ponies and donkeys are finally beginning to work once more?"

Everyone looks at Griffin, who has deliberately broken the tension.

"The ponies?" asks Elaine.

"Aye, the pit ponies," answers Griffin.

"What happened to them?" asks Amy.

"Well see, it wasn't what happened to the ponies like, it was what happened to the miners that caused all the problems, in it."

"What was that?" asks Faith.

Bernard knows the story and so starts tucking into his slowed-cooked lamb with gusto.

"Well ew see, since this yer diwygiad happened the men have stopped their cussing and blaspheming and turned to more genteel language." He scoops a few hurried spoons of food into his mouth before looking up again. Puzzled faces look back at him. Chuckling, he takes his time savoring the cawl. Then looking up, he finds all eyes are still on him, as they wait to hear the rest.

"Any lady can go down the pit now and not blush, not even once, for hearing something offensive she will not."

"Ack-uh-vee! What about the donkeys?" demands Eva.

"Well, it's like they all went deaf, see. No matter how many times they was politely asked to move, the stubborn mules refused to budge. Like statues they became, so they did, like fine pieces of art in a grand museum."

"What was wrong with them?" asks Amy.

"They didn't understand the instructions anymore, see. They were so used to cussing to get them moving, that they no longer understood the miners, who have all had their mouths washed out with heavenly soap!"

There is the slightest pause before everyone around the table starts laughing.

"'Tis the truth I speak, so I do. It's taken months to re-train them to obey new instructions. They did put the colliery right behind on its production schedules. Even Laird Anderson has come to visit the mines to find out what was happening."

There is no need to explain who Anderson is, for a lot of the collieries in South Wales belong to the Scotsman.

"I surely would have liked to be down those mines. Watching the miners trying to make the donkeys move must have been a funny sight," says Amy.

"Aye, 'tis indeed a *funny* thing this diwygiad, a touching and a changing a person it be, and all for the better. Have ew not seen a change in your own daughters, Bernard?" Although Griffin is asking the butcher a question, his eyes are fixed firmly on Faith.

Feeling his stare, she can ignore it no longer and lifts her head to look back at him. His leather-like, sun-kissed face, full of wrinkles and blemishes, looks back at her with somber austerity. Knowing eyes study her over a huge bulbous red nose. She feels uncomfortable and fidgets in her seat.

"Now that ew should mention it, I have! I thought it was Mrs Miller's good influence over them, but to be honest like, I think they've been changing since this year past. Yes, yes indeed, now I consider it, it's been ever since they first went to listen to that young Evan Roberts, when he was preaching over in Cardiff." Bernard regards his daughters who are all looking at him with love. His eyes swim with emotion. "I didn't hear ew," he whispers.

Amy jumps up and comes behind him, giving him a huge hug. "'Tis not us ew had to hear, Pa. Ew wouldn't know until ew felt the Lord yourself."

He pats her hand, not ashamed to embrace in public, as he had been but a month ago. "'Tis full of joy ew all have been," says Bernard.

Amy gives him a kiss on his cheek, before going back to her seat.

"Now I tell ew the truth," continues Griffin, "since a young lad a Christian I have been. Faithful all my days in the best way I knew how." He continues looking directly at Faith, who puts down her spoon, finding herself getting lost in his deep rich accent.

"But since this yer movement of Duw has swept through Wales like a tidal wave, I have been a changed man. Oh, and 'tis praying I be, that I'll never change back. All my doubts and my questionings have been dispersed as the joy and the peace of Duw has soothed my soul. Yet, I am a weak man and my sins do plague me still, even amid this glorious movement. Should be easy, should it not, for a man on fire to remain true and good? Nothing good comes easy ew mark my words, for something worth having often requires some sort of sacrifice."

Faith develops a lump in throat. Scrunching up her toes she tries fighting back the emotions that are battling to be released.

"Do ew know when I was in Ebenzer's a few months back, I heard the Rev. D Collier say, 'the mistakes in his life had been many but, praise be to God, who declares that we are truly loved and truly forgiven'. Aye, since that sermon I tell ew, Psalm 103 has become most precious to me. For it states that...

> *He does not treat us as our sins deserve or repay us according to our iniquities. For as high as the heavens are above the earth, so great is His love for those who fear Him.*

Forgiveness is most precious, but not only to offering it unto others but in accepting it for ourselves."

Faith pushes her chair back and squeezes words out of a tight throat. "I need to get back. I don't want to be walking in the dark. Night everyone, I will see you in two weeks at the wedding."

"Nos da chi," the sisters say with worry filled eyes.

"Nos da chi, Faith bach," says Bernard, watching her as she hastens to the door.

"Faith, stay," cries Bertie, climbing down from his chair and running after her, his little chin wobbling.

She leans down and cups his face in her hands and puts on her gentlest smile. "I will be back soon." She kisses his forehead. "You be good now."

Eva comes over and picks him up. "Will ew sleep with me tonight, my little man?"

All dejection is gone in a split second. "Will ew sing to me?"

"Oh aye, yes I will."

Faith catches a sob in her mouth, and turning she flees before it can escape. *I should be singing to him. It's me who should tuck him into his bed, me, me, me.*

"Faith?"

Faith stops in her tracks on the road and turns to face her mother. No words come, just tears. Nell rushes forward and gathers Faith in her arms.

"Oh, my love," Nell whispers over and over, until the crying fades.

"I have to go, Mam."

"You won't delay in coming, will you? I couldn't be happy on my wedding day unless you are here and happy with me."

"I'll not delay."

Nell wipes the tear stains off Faith's face.

"You know you mean the world to me?"

"Yes, Mam, as you are to me."

Nell watches her daughter until she turns off the road onto the lane that leads to Driscoll. "Lord, in your mercy, please watch over my little girl."

In the golden light of the day's last hour, as the hills set to glowing red with the residue rays of the setting sun, Geoffrey is standing on the edge of the lane. His body is silhouetted black and mysterious against the tall hedgerow as fear gnaws in his guts. She should have returned by now. He moves from foot to foot, to circulate his blood. Numbness is an indicator of how long he's been waiting for her.

Movement catches his eye, and he strains forward. Yes, there's no mistaking the lithe body of Faith, as she painstakingly ambles her way home. Overcome with relief he charges down the lane to greet her. The closer he gets the more he slows down, becoming aware of her distress.

"Faith, what's wrong?"

She takes a quick peek at him. Her face is red and blotchy, eyes swollen and sore looking, and he realizes the amount of crying she's done is great.

"Faith?" He opens his arms for her, and she flies into them, his arms clasping tightly around her body. Holding her to him, he wonders what dreadful event could have befallen her. She's past crying, but holds onto Geoffrey as one full of sorrow and need. His strength and warmth are comforting, dissolving her internal pain (created by a spirit at war with itself). In this silent moment of comfort, Faith knows that Geoffrey loves her and the warmth from that knowledge radiates through her.

After some time, as the birds sing out their eventide song, Faith takes a step backwards out of his embrace. "You were watching for me?"

"You have been on mind all evening, and I confess a panic that you were in trouble rose within me. I am glad to find you, but tell me, what has happened to vex you so?"

"Can we walk?"

"Yes, of course." He reaches out, taking hold of her hand as they start back towards Driscoll. Knowing there isn't much time left, she decides to share with him just a little of what bothers her.

"Do you know how hard it is to be surrounded by believers, when you yourself cannot find it within you to believe?"

"I was raised a Christian, Faith, so I don't know exactly how you feel but I can imagine."

"I feel that everyone condemns me for not believing in God."

"That is not true, let me assure you. No one condemns you. Everyone is entitled to believe or not. Only God can call you and only God can fully understand the person you are. If anyone judges you for lack of belief I would be the first to chide their unchristian ways."

"What if I can't see Him because I am too wicked, and He doesn't want me? What if my unbelief is my entire fault?"

"Faith." Geoffrey stops walking, pulling her to his side so he can look into her eyes. "How can you say such a thing about yourself? I don't understand why you would think that. You are a lovely person, there is nothing wicked about you."

Her bottom jaw juts to the side and then she snaps it shut tight. She will not share her dark secret with him and watch the love he has for her die. She would rather spend eternity on her own than let the shame and disgrace of her past be known to him. She has never considered herself proud, but in this moment she realizes that her pride will never let her reveal the truth to him.

"We need to return and it wouldn't be good for anyone to see us this close. Please go ahead and I will follow at my own speed."

Rejection again! Geoffrey doesn't know what to do with her, how can he help her when she continually pushes him away? When she had fallen into his arms happiness sprung forth, filling him with hope that she would accept him. Now, here she is yet again putting a barrier between them.

"You go ahead, I wish to walk a little while longer."

She searches his face and seeing his pain, once again feels sick inside for hurting him. But resolve she has aplenty. She has been laughed at, scorned, tarnished and discarded in her past, and never again will she let anyone do that to her. She sets off ahead of him, teeth gritted in determination. *Never, never again.*

Geoffrey watches until she is safely in the courtyard and then sets off across the fields. As he marches he prays for wisdom and understanding.

Chapter 10

For once in her life, Faith can sympathize with women who profess to suffer from 'ladies illnesses' where fatigue and prostration mean they are confined to the couch! Never before has she felt so mentally exhausted, and yet she is as full of optimism as if to burst a dam of joy.

During the last two weeks, Geoffrey has appeared to talk to her several times. Mostly on her afternoon break when she likes to sit in the sun on the hill and look towards the black smoke that rises in the distance, pinpointing Abertillery. If she closes her eyes she can imagine the hustle and bustle of the mining town with its constant rumbling and hissing of steam that comes from the engine houses. Every now and again she can see smoke rising and hear the chug-chug of the trains as they carry the coal away.

At first, she had been uncomfortable, wondering what the staff might think, but although they had been spotted together numerous times, no one mentioned anything. They were only talking, after all, hardly anything to make a fuss about, she told herself.

Geoffrey had taken to talking about everything and anything, mostly to do with the management of the house and grounds. He often went into great lengths explaining how it all worked and how much they relied on the rent from the farmers to pay the bills at Driscoll. Not once did he mention his feelings towards her, nor did he ever touch her or ask her awkward questions. As the days slipped by she began to relax and to enjoy his company and their friendship grew.

Today, however, the staff *did* have something to say when they discovered that Lord Driscoll is taking her into town for her mother's wedding - in his carriage. He told the housekeeper he was going that way anyway and was indeed himself delivering Faith to Nell in one piece so that she might enjoy the day and not be tired. Cook muttered several times, in a not so quiet voice, something about eggs and stones, while Mrs Lewis had quite openly tutted for all to hear. As for Reuben, his red face and the slamming of doors has made Faith realize that today is actually a step too far. Too late to do anything about it now though, as they are already sitting side-by-side in the springy carriage.

Discomfort from the staff's open disapproval has dissolved the happiness she had that today is her mother's wedding day. The closeness of Geoffrey is also taking her mind off the special day. All she can think about is how soft his lips look, wondering what they would feel like pressed against her own. Longing, to reach out and take hold of his hand, fills her. Glancing at his long fingers and well-manicured nails, she closes her eyes briefly, imagining his touch. When she opens them again she finds him watching her with a tender smile. Her face flushes hot, and she's afraid he might have read her thoughts.

"I'll be visiting friends for most of the day, but would you mind if on my way back I stop by to see if you're ready to return?"

"I don't know what time it will finish. I'm sure it won't be until after seven o'clock, though."

"That's fine, I'll check in on you and if you're not ready I will go back to Driscoll without you."

"As you wish."

The rest of the journey is done in a comfortable silence, both wrapped up in their own thoughts. Faith gazes out of the window and wishes that she could undo time. Go back and put her mistakes to right. She never would have given Harrison a chance to even talk to her if she had known what he was like. Just as she is confirming to herself that she would have stayed well away from him the image of Bertie comes to her. Her spirit melts, for if she were to undo the past then Bertie would not be here. Sighing, she leans back into the cushioned seat. No, the past would just have to stay the way it was because she wouldn't change a thing if it meant she didn't have her son.

Fred, who has stepped in to drive the coach as Ivor (the stable master come coachman) isn't feeling so hearty, opens the door and offers Faith his hand. She feels awkward but accepts his assistance in climbing down the huge step.

With her feet firmly on the ground she looks up and smiles at him. "Thank you, Fred."

Fred, however, stands by the side of the door and acts as if he hasn't heard her. The rejection cuts deep and Faith drops her gaze downwards, not knowing what to do.

"Have a good day, Faith, and please pass on my congratulations to your mother and Mr Morgan."

Faith gives Geoffrey a weak attempt at a smile and as she turns away she hears Fred close the door and climb back up onto the box. She resists turning around to see if Geoffrey's watching her. If she had, she would have been disappointed, because not wanting to draw any attention to them he remains well back in his seat.

"Faith, Faith we're having a celebration!" Bertie charges across the room as soon as she opens the door, throwing himself into her arms. Picking him up, she swings him around, making him laugh.

"Where's Mam?" Faith asks Eva, who is rigorously rubbing Bertie's shoes with a cloth to make them shine.

"She came over all a flutter and took to her bed."

"Oh, no." Faith puts Bertie down and rushes towards the stairs.

"She said she was just feeling a little faint. 'Tis probably all the excitement," sighs Eva. "I tell ew the truth see. I would surely be overcome with many a swooning spell, if it was my wedding day."

Taking the stairs two at a time, Faith hears Amy's reply.

"Heaven's above, if it was your wedding day I would be fainting and keeling over for to be honest like, I would be so shocked that some poor man with no brains between his ears should have proposed to ew!"

"Hey!" There's a thump as Eva throws a cloth at Amy, which is followed by girlie giggles.

"My turn," shouts Bertie grabbing a shoe cloth. A tussle follows as the girls chase him around the room.

"Mam?"

Nell opens her eyes, and seeing Faith, smiles as she reaches out to her. "'Tis good to see you, my love."

"Are you unwell?"

"No, I'm fine." Nell taps the bed. "Come and lie with me for a while."

Faith lies down next to her mother, as she used to do when she was little, and Nell wraps her arm around her.

"Tell me, are you happy?"

Faith is a little surprised by the question. "Yes, Mam, life is good to us, is it not? And you're to be married today, becoming the butcher's wife an all. I was thinking if you get married again you'll have to look for a candlestick maker!"

Nell's smile doesn't reach her eyes.

Faith leans on her elbow and looks across at her. "Mam, you're beginning to worry me. What's wrong?"

Nell reaches up and strokes Faith's face. "You're beautiful, you know that?"

Faith blushes.

"It's not surprising that Lord Driscoll has taken a fancy to you."

Faith sits up, her face now as hot as burning coals.

"Oh, don't you try and deny it," says Nell sitting up as well. "'Tis the talk of the town you are now, so you are."

"We've not done anything wrong, we only talk. We're just friends, nothing more."

"I don't doubt it, Faith."

They sit side-by-side on the bed. Crushing silence fills the room, and Faith feels her ears might burst from it.

"We've done nothing wrong, Mam. I wouldn't shame you again, I promise you I wouldn't."

Nell wraps her fingers through Faith's curls, giving them a gentle squeeze. "You might not have done anything, but tongues are a wagging. Many a shrewish maiden has nodded in my direction with that look of knowing disgrace. You should know better than to give witches cause to stir the cauldron, for what bitter brew they serve when gossip is in the pot."

"Oh, Mam, I'm full of sorrowful frustrations. I'm not going to lie to you see, never have I encouraged him and often I have spurned him, honest like."

"Faith Miller, as I live and breathe, you're turning Welsh!"

Their eyes seek each other out, and then they're laughing. It starts gently but soon turns into uncontrollable belly-aching laughter.

When they finally get control back, Nell wipes her eyes with the back of her arm. Looking at Faith with a serious, yet gently imploring stare, she urges, "You'll tell him he is to desist in his advances or you will leave."

For a moment the smile falls from Faith's eyes, but she knows that what Nell's saying is right. "I will."

The service is short and sweet but made memorable by both the Six Bells Colliery, and the Abertillery Police male choirs. The police choir of six – the total number of policemen for the valley, had been paid to sing in church, whereas the Six Bells choir had come as a surprise, lining the street outside of Ebenezer's as the couple came out.

Reuben for weeks had been collecting the heads off the rose bushes around Driscoll's gardens before they fell and Faith had gently pulled the petals apart, letting them dry. Now as her mother and new husband come out of the church, both beaming broadly, all the girls are able to throw the petals over them.

Faith lifts Bertie up so he can throw some too, but as soon as his are gone he turns his face up to Faith and grumpily declares, "I'm hungry."

Faith is just about to reassure him that they will eat soon, when Eva turns around and offers him a pork pie. His eyes light up as he accepts it.

"Ta, Eeeva," he says with his mouth full.

Faith puts him down but holds his hand, keeping him close. Watching him scoff the pie makes her wonder if the memory of being hungry will ever leave him. Looking up once more, she catches Bernard watching her.

"I'll take right good care of the boy, Faith, I promise ew."

A lump forms into her throat and for a moment she feels as if he knows that Bertie's her son. Turning her gaze to her mother, who's accepting congratulations from most of the town's women folk, she just knows she'd never reveal the truth.

Faith is amazed at how many people pour in and out of the butchers that day, all celebrating with copious amounts of jubilant singing, dancing, eating, and even a little drinking.

The folk of Abertillery are indeed a changed community. Even a year back a wedding would have been a good excuse for partaking in too much beer and maybe a whiskey or two. Today, however, only a few old die-hards who said they'd risk meeting the devil rather than give up liquor are still swilling it back. Despite the lack of drinking the day is the gayest Faith has ever experienced. She soon gets used to the burly miners breaking into song and the women all gooey-eyed as they listen to their strapping husbands. And, despite her resolve not to draw close to God, she finds herself joining in with the hymns.

Here is love, vast as the ocean has been sung so many times in the last year that Faith often finds herself humming the tune, even when trying to go to sleep. The song of love seems to have drenched the valley with its powerful peace as it hangs in the air and is carried in the wind like golden snowflakes of tenderness.

She has sat and listened to many a conversation throughout the day and has to admit that this diwygiad has certainly had an impact on the town, one that no one can deny. Reporters from all around the world had arrived in various towns across Wales and were reporting back on this remarkable movement of God.

"Ew should a seen 'is face, I tell ew," laughs PC Thomas. "It's third time, 'ees bin ina' court room and not a person for him to judge."

"The last time we had anyone up before the magistrate was Mr Sullivan, was it not?" says PS Stanfield.

"That's reet, poor James Sullivan and all because he was playing pitch-and-toss in Green Row on a Sunday," answers PC Thomas. "Got fined a full half-a-crown an' all 'ee did."

"Too right to," interjects old Griffin, waving his finger in the air for good measure.

"I'll ew the truth, thought we was for the chop when he asked us why the town should have six Bobbies, when ne'er a crime's being committed," continued PC Thomas.

"He went purple he did, when he came to the station and found out it was empty, because we'd been hired out to sing at a funeral service," said PS Stanfield. "Said we was ripping off the Crown. Took lots of persuasion and convincing for him to believe we was raising money for the widows fund, it did."

"What did you say?" asks Faith.

"We offered to pray for him," answers PS Stanfield with elaborated seriousness. "He soon shot off out through the door after that." There's a moment's silence and then the room erupts in laughter.

Faith shakes her head and moves away, leaving the double act to continue with their stories.

Searching the room, she spots Bertie resting his head on Eva's chest as she rocks him to sleep. Jealousy flares vivid-red through her chest and out her nostrils as she crosses the room, swiftly passing through the thick set of bodies.

"I'll take him."

Eva looks at Faith's outstretched arms and smiles with understanding far outweighing her years. She carefully prises Bertie off her body and hands him over, all the time her eyes oozing loving kindness.

Faith makes her way through the jolly crowd again and heads up the stairs. Bertie has a small cot made up on the floor besides Eva and Amy's bed, but as Faith goes to lay him down she changes her mind. Sitting on Amy's bed she cradles him tightly to her. Rocking gently, she hums to him as she's done since he was born. Shadows of sorrow and melancholy swirl around her mind. It isn't until she becomes aware that Bertie is cold that she lays him down, covering him up with a motherly tuck.

"I wish for you all the happiness I could never give you. May your life be rich and full of love. Know this, my sweet boy, I would lay down my life for you in an instant."

Her steps down the stairs are heavy and slow and she forces herself to smile as she enters the room, which is at last starting to empty. Force of habit takes her to the kitchen where she ties on an apron and begins washing up the dirty dishes.

"Here."

She turns around to see Nell holding out a glass to her, its contents rich in color like honey. Wiping her hands on the apron she attempts a smile, but Nell sees only dull eyes.

"Diolch." *(Thank you)* Faith takes the glass, tapping it against her mother's, before taking a big gulp.

"Welsh?"

"Well, Bernard's very good and speaks English most of the time, but I know he loves to exchange conversation in his own language. I think you might want to brush up on your Welsh. I'm sure it would please him mightily."

Nell sips her drink, observing her daughter closely. "Are you going to be all right?"

Faith pulls a face. "Course I am. I'm well looked after at the manor."

"There will be space here for you one day, you know that, don't you?"

"Yes, Mam, don't worry about me."

Nell swills her drink around for a moment, paying it all her attention before looking up at Faith. "He's here, you know."

"Who is?"

"Lord Driscoll."

"Really?" Faith spins around, half expecting to find Geoffrey standing behind her.

"He's been waiting well past an hour now."

"Really!" Faith is shocked. "Why didn't you tell me?"

"You were upstairs with Bertie."

Faith looks into the golden liquid in her glass before knocking it back. "I best not keep him waiting any longer then." Exchanging her apron for her shawl, she heads for the door.

"Faith?"

"It's fine. I promise you nothing will happen." Faith comes back and throws her arms around Nell, holding her tight. Nell returns the hug.

"It was a lovely day, I'm so happy for you both." Before she starts crying on the evening of her mother's wedding day, Faith spins around and hastens out of the back door. Spotting the carriage straight away, she rushes towards it. She needs to be in her own room, where no one but Olwen can hear her cry. Opening the door, she starts climbing in before Fred has a chance to get down and help her.

Geoffrey leans forward and offers his hand to help her up. Taking one look at her face, he knows she doesn't want to talk. Tapping on the roof with his cane he calls out, "Home now, Fred."

The carriage moves off before Faith has sat back in the seat, and she's thrown forward. Geoffrey catches her and instead of releasing her he pulls her protectively into his arms. She's too tired and sad to fight off the thing she most wants in the world, so she sinks into his arms and lays her head upon his chest. Strong arms envelop and hold her tight, making her feel safe and secure. The fact that he offers no conversation, instinctively knowing what she needs, warms her heart more than anything else could do. Despite wanting to wait until she is in the safety of her own bed, the tears begin to flow.

Geoffrey pulls out his handkerchief and offers it to her and after accepting it she buries her face in the crisp white cotton. The smell of soap wafts up from the cloth which, along with the comfort of his embrace, soothes her. Long before they reach home she's calm and the crying has stopped.

When they reach the front entrance of the manor, Fred jumps down and opens the door. "The kitchen door has been left unlocked for you, Faith."

"Thank you, Fred, nos da *(goodnight)*."

Fred nods at her and then Geoffrey. "Nos da, m'lord."

"Goodnight Fred, and thank you for staying out so late."

As Fred leads the horse and carriage towards the stables, Faith tips her head back so she can look at Geoffrey.

"Thank you for waiting for me, and thank you for the handkerchief. I will have it laundered and return it to you promptly."

Geoffrey takes her hand that clutches the cloth and wraps both his hands around it. "There's no need to return it. I have a drawer full of them and no need for them except to adorn my suits. Besides, I feel you have a far greater need of it than me."

His eyes are smiling and for a moment Faith feels the love pouring from them. She snatches her hand back and takes a step backwards. "Goodnight m'lord." She turns and with a quick pace sets off for the back of the house and the kitchen entrance.

Chapter 11

"What say you, Mrs Lewis?"

"About what?"

"It says yer," says Cook tapping the newspaper, "that Mrs S. A. Allen's World's Hair Restorer can change white or gray hair to its natural color and that it never fails."

"Goodness, Mrs Jones, do tell me that you are not so gullible?" The housekeeper peers over her glasses at Cook in dismay.

"Well." Cook pats her dark gray bun. "I wouldn't mind being brown again, and that's the truth."

"Sincere I am, and out of respect I do say this, vanity blossoms but bears no fruit."

"Oh, go on away with ew, Mrs Lewis, 'tis only speculating I be. When do I have time to fancy m'self up like?"

Faith smiles into the bucket of potatoes she's peeling. She'd grown to love the friendly banter between the staff and is at last beginning to feel truly accepted. It has helped that Geoffrey is once more in London and has been for the last three weeks. It is more comfortable knowing he wouldn't be seeking her out as she was beginning to wonder how much longer she could resist his advances.

"Mrs Jones, do you think you could spare Faith for a few hours today?"

Faith looks over at the housekeeper in surprise. *What does she want with me?*

Cook shifts uncomfortably in her chair for a moment as she pretends to scrutinize an article in the paper, thus giving herself time to compose an answer. For in truth, Faith has started taking over many of Cook's bothersome chores, and if she were to go with Mrs Lewis, then Cook would have to do them herself. She sighs, seeing no way around it.

"Of course, Mrs Lewis," is her polite response as she carefully folds the huge newspaper. "Maybe after two?"

"Perfect. Faith, I'll see you at two sharply."

"Yes, Mrs Lewis."

Exiting the kitchen with a straight back and a jingle of keys, the housekeeper doesn't see the puzzled looks exchanged by Faith and Cook.

"Guess we'll find out soon enough, now get a move on with those tatties as I need you to pluck the goose before you go. You'll need time to change and wash too, 'cause for sure she'll want you spic and span for whatever task she has in mind for you."

Faith follows the housekeeper down the corridor. A flutter of excitement bubbles inside her as she's not seen more of the house than her room, the kitchen and the corridors in-between. Esther and Olwen clean the house with Mrs Lewis's beady eye overseeing all that is done. She crosses her fingers behind her back, hoping that they're going to clean the library.

Disappointingly, they don't go far and stop in the grand dining room. There is a smaller dining room, she'd heard, where the Driscolls usually eat. To her knowledge this room has not been used since she arrived.

Mrs Lewis walks around to the other side of a huge table, indicating that Faith should stand on the opposite side. Together they start rolling back the heavy linen cloth, revealing the beautiful rich walnut tones beneath. They work together in silence as they fold the cloth into a neat square.

Faith traces a finger along the wood. "It's beautiful."

"The table needs polishing. Have you used linseed varnish before?"

Faith shakes her head.

"You use very little oil and the lightest touch. I mean… the *lightest* touch, do you understand?"

"Yes, Mrs Lewis."

The housekeeper unscrews the tin and pours the smallest amount of oil onto the corner of a cloth. "With the softest of touches you rub the oil in a small area, like so. Then you take a clean cloth and in a swirling motion, light as a feather's touch, you polish until the oil is no more. Then you move on to the next piece. Not a single mark should remain. When the sun glances over the table tomorrow afternoon it should look like glass."

Mrs Lewis straightens up, her hands clasped together at her waist line as she watches Faith start polishing. She examines the work so intently that sweat breaks out on Faith's forehead. Finally, satisfied she can be trusted with the task, the housekeeper walks towards the door, then as an afterthought she turns around.

"This divider also needs polishing. I will have the library ladders brought in for you so you can reach the top." With that she spins around once again, and with a swish of her skirt is gone.

Faith gapes at the divider in horror. It is massive, nearly as high as the ceiling, and almost as wide as the room. There's just enough space on either side of it for the servants to walk around when passing into the corridor on the way to the kitchen. The oak screen is impressively big and heavy and beautifully ornate with hunting scenes and flowers worked throughout the surface, but as she studies the intricate carvings she realizes the enormity of the task in front of her. Done properly, it could take a week!

Faith is only on her third section of the table when the housekeeper returns with Mr Humphries in tow, carrying some ladders. The estate steward gives Mrs Lewis an odd look when it becomes obvious to him that Faith is expected to polish it on her own.

"Shall I fetch Olwen, do ew think, Mrs Lewis?" he says scratching his head.

"No, she is busy preparing the hall for dancing."

"As you say," replies Mr Humphries with a nod, before leaving.

"Is there to be a party?" asks Faith.

"Yes indeed, a very grand affair. One which has not been seen in the manor since the late Lord Driscoll passed on. Miss Margaret is throwing a surprise birthday party for her brother. She has informed me that all the eligible ladies in South Wales will be attending and it is her intention that she should find him a suitable wife, one that can be mistress of this fine home and bring it some dignity and elegance."

Faith knows the housekeeper isn't prone to gossip, nor is she ever heard referring to Lord and Lady Driscoll as Miss Margaret and her brother. It is quite out of character for her. It therefore leaves Faith in no doubt whatsoever that she is passing on more than information. She is, in fact, reminding Faith that Geoffrey is far above her. As far apart as a bird soaring in the sky to a worm burrowing in the earth, is the lowly maid to the Lord of the Manor.

Faith knows in her bones that Geoffrey wants more than dignity and elegance, he needs, nay desires, love and tenderness. She isn't too sure he will find it in fancy frills, fluttering fans and empty conversation. No sooner has the thought entered her mind than she chides herself. Looking down at the table she resumes polishing, for of course there will be lovely, kind ladies who might attend as well, women with character such as Margaret herself.

Concentrating on the table isn't enough to prevent her thoughts being full of Geoffrey. If – no, when – he chooses a bride she will be heartbroken, for she can deny the truth no more, she is totally in love with him.

Shaking her head doesn't disperse the image of his face from her mind. Chewing her bottom lip, she blinks, trying to stay the tears that threaten to come. It wouldn't be good to let the housekeeper guess why she's upset.

Content the kitchen maid is not only doing a good job but that she also knows her place, Mrs Lewis waltzes out, finally leaving Faith on her own.

Her right shoulder is aching by the time she finishes the table and she scowls at the room divider in dismay. It will be practically impossible to get this done before she is needed back in the kitchen.

Picking up a pile of clean cloths and the tin of oil, she climbs the steps, placing the items in the small box on top of the ladders, and starts polishing what is seriously one of the most spectacular things she's ever seen.

Clueless to how long she has been polishing, having only managed the top third of screen, she gives way to tears of pain. Her arm feels so sore she isn't sure she'll ever be able to lift it again. Just in that moment, Esther and Olwen come running in. They see her tearful face, but instead of making a fuss they simply pick up cloths, ask for the oil to be passed down and start polishing the bottom of the divider.

After a while of working in companionable silence, Olwen begins quietly singing hymns. At first, she sings ones that Faith doesn't know, but as she grows in confidence and sings a bit louder, Faith is overcome with a shiver and interrupts her.

"Olwen, will you sing that hymn about oceans?"

"Here is love vast as the ocean…" Listening to her friend sing, Faith is filled with emotions she can't describe and, without thinking, joins in.

"Loving kindness as the flood…"

On the third line Esther also joins in. *"When the Prince of Life our ransom, shed for us His precious blood."*

"Who His love will not remember…" the three girls turn around to see who has just joined in and find Lady Driscoll standing in the doorway.

"Please, don't stop," says Margaret coming into the room.

Olwen and Esther carry on singing along with Lady Driscoll, but Faith's in awe and can't open her mouth. Margaret's wearing the prettiest dress Faith has ever seen. Cream silk with lace over the top, all along the short sleeves and neckline are rows of pearls making it look like the dress is adorned with flowers. Margaret's soft brown hair is piled on top of her head, making her look simply stunning.

When they finish the song, Lady Driscoll inspects the screen they've just about finished. "It will be good to use this room again, and to hear it full of chatter and laughter. Oh, how I've missed the company of good friends. Is the hall ready, Olwen?"

"Yes indeed, milady," answers Olwen with a curtsy.

Just then, the housekeeper comes marching brusquely into the room.

"Ah, Mrs Lewis, just the person I need. Come with me, please."

Mrs Lewis nods and starts to follow Lady Driscoll out of the room but as she goes she throws a frown over her shoulder at the girls. Once they are sure she is out of earshot Olwen pulls a face.

"We'll probably be in for it now."

"For helping me?" Faith asks.

"No, for singing in the house," replies Esther. "Come on, let's get back to the kitchen, we're all done here."

Lord Driscoll came back early, and with the party no longer being a surprise the preparations are made without delay. Fresh flower garlands arrive in the afternoon and hang over all the door frames, filling the house with the amazing smells of chrysanthemum, rose and lavender.

All the servants are pulled together for a couple of hours to polish the silver which will be on display. Not that the party will be enjoyed by them, yet still it buoyed their spirits, so everyone is in good cheer. They work late into the night making sure everything is exactly how Lady Driscoll desires, meaning all fall into their beds in complete exhaustion.

Faith is the first one up as normal and sets about lighting the huge kitchen stoves and making the dough for the day's bread. Her right shoulder still aches from the polishing and so kneading the dough is tough going. One by one the staff come into the kitchen rubbing their eyes, seeking a cup of tea to start their day off with.

Early chores complete, it is with relief that they pile around the table to have breakfast. The bread is still hot from the oven. Faith spreads honey over hers and sinks her teeth into it. Giving an appreciative moan she thinks she's died and gone to heaven, it is that tasty.

"Something smells awfully good in here." Everyone pushes their chairs back and stand smartly as Lord Driscoll approaches. "Please, carry on with your breakfast." Somewhat hesitantly, they sit back down. "I think I will join you."

"Salutations to ew, Lord Driscoll." Ivor tips his finger to his forehead as he speaks. The rest of the staff add their birthday wishes with gusto.

"Thank you, and I am sorry if my sister has used my birthday to pile more jobs on you. I hope it hasn't been too overbearing?"

"Eee 'tis a pleasure m'lord," says Cook beaming.

Esther's eyes nearly pop out of her head as Lord Driscoll squeezes himself onto the end of the bench next to Faith. Faith stiffens, her hand half-way to her mouth. She sits like a statue, with no idea what to do.

Geoffrey nudges her with his elbow. "Tuck in, Faith, you're as skinny as a rake." Olwen rushes to fetch a plate and cup for him, which he accepts from her with a large grin. "Now come along, eat up everyone, doubtless you have loads to do today, so please eat away." He sees their hesitation, so cuts a large slice of bread, puts some cheese on it and starts eating. This is the signal they needed to carry on breaking their fast.

Faith, with shaking hand, brings the bread to her mouth and takes a small bite.

"You mustn't blame me for joining you, how could I resist the smell of such wonderful bread. Cook, you deserve a medal, this is quite delicious!"

"Actually, m'lord, it was Faith who baked the bread today."

Geoffrey raises an eyebrow in response to Cook and then turns to look at Faith. "You have a talent, Faith."

"Thank you, m'lord."

Finally, everyone relaxes and with Geoffrey's encouragement continue not only with breakfast but after a short silence pick up their normal chatter.

"Not being funny like, but 'tis sure I am that them blasted fairies have been at the vegetable patch again."

"Reuben ew be speaking through yer hat again!" exclaims Esther.

"Maybe not," says Cook refilling her teacup. "I've grown up with many a tale about the fairies and their magical music, which everyone agrees is low and pleasant, but none can ever remember the tune to sing it themselves."

"I find it impossible to believe in something I cannot see," says Faith.

Geoffrey glances down at her but says nothing.

"I saw them, you see, when I was young." Everyone stops eating and stare at Mr Humphries. "'Twas the music, sweet and mellow, that called me from my sleep and led me out into the forest."

"Ew never went a venturing after them?" cries Olwen in shock.

"Weren't sure who was playing was I? It just sounded so enchanting and I had to find out who could sing like that."

"What did ew see?" asks Esther leaning forward over the table.

"Well fairies seem not to delight in open plains or near water, but they do seem to dwell in dry grounds, not far from trees and hedges and liking the shade of fully grown trees, the oak especially. But, I tell ew the truth, I ventured into them trees with expectation of coming upon the camp of gypsies. Never was a boy more surprised than me, when I came across a fairy gathering within a mushroom circle."

"Ach, go on with you, don't you be telling such tall tales," interrupts Cook.

"As Duw is my witness, I am only telling ew what my eyes saw and my ears heard."

"What did they do when they saw ew?" asks Esther with wide eyes.

"Asked me if I wanted to join them they did, however, they did also mention that to do so I must first die, 'cos only the spirit can sing and dance with fairies see."

Both Olwen and Esther gasp, and Faith rolls her eyes.

"Were you tempted to join them?" asks Geoffrey, eyes sparkling with humor.

"Not on 'yer life! I high-tailed it home as fast as me skinny little pins would take me. Next day was my fifth birthday and me pa had promised to take me fishing for the day."

Most around the table find it hard to believe that the gentle giant had ever been small with thin legs. The image makes them laugh.

"They must be horrid indeed if they wanted ew to die," mulls Esther.

"Indeed!" agrees Olwen.

"I don't believe they be as wicked as the ghosts. Now… they really *do* want ew dead!"

Olwen and Esther gasp again.

"Reuben!" snaps Cook.

"Well 'tis true, in it. Too many a person now, has spotted the ghost along Aberbeeg Road, that chases them as if to kill them, and that's no lie."

"Why would ghosts want us dead?" asks Olwen in a tiny voice.

"Because they're proper sour in death's condition, they won't move on to the next place, their bitterness and anger anchors them to the ground."

"And if ever there was a reason for us to learn the art of forgiveness then there it is," declares the housekeeper standing up. "Now, enough story-telling, come, there is much to be done today."

Needing no second telling everyone shoots up and starts clearing the table. Faith goes to the sink and starts washing the first round of dishes, in a day that promises to be full of a plethora of dishes requiring cleaning.

Geoffrey brings his plate over and puts in on the drainer next to her.

"Thank you, m'lord."

"Is that all you can say to me today?" His voice is the quietest whisper meant only for her ears. It sends shivers of desire down her back.

"I wish you many congratulations of the day, m'lord and do sincerely hope you have a splendid time at your party. I hear a band is coming up from Swansea and that you will be dancing in the hall."

"I won't be dancing."

"You won't?"

"There is only one woman I wish to have in my arms, and if she would only return my love I would be the happiest man alive. So no, as it stands I will not be dancing today."

Before Faith can think of anything to say he has turned, leaving her in a state of shock surrounded by plates and pans, and full of disturbing longings.

There is so much to be done that it is evening before Faith knows it. She is shocked at the amount of food that has to be prepared to feed fifty or so people. Having never seen such a huge spread in her life she can't help thinking that it is enough food to feed an army.

Near the end of the night, when all the eating is finished and a few people have left, the servants sit down to a meal of such magnificence that it takes Faith's breath away. Her favorite, by far, is Cook's honey roasted ham which simply melts in her mouth. They are exhausted so there isn't much chatter around the table. They all seem content to just listen to the band's melodic tunes as they float through the house.

The grandfather clock in the hall had struck twelve a while back. The band, who have finished packing their instruments away, are making their way out of the room as Faith, Olwen and Esther enter to do the last of the cleaning-up. In a state of reverie, Faith moves around the room, absorbing the impressive portraits on the wall, and the breath-taking mural on the ceiling.

"Come on you, or we'll never get to bed." Olwen smiles at her.

Back in the kitchen for the last time, everyone is yawning and agrees it's time for bed.

Faith pours hot water from the kettle into the sink. "I'll just finish washing these glasses and then I'll come up."

"Don't be long, Faith bach, we still have to be up early tomorrow," says Cook as bent over, she shuffles out of the kitchen, displaying her aches and pains.

It doesn't take Faith long to finish the last of the glasses, and she is soon going around the kitchen turning off the gas lamps. Coming out of the kitchen and into the hall she stops. She should turn left and go up the stairs to her room, but she feels a pull to return to the hall. Faith tiptoes along the corridor, not that anyone would hear her, and gently pushes open the floor to ceiling doors that open up into the hall.

She lights the table lamp, although the moon light is probably enough to study the paintings. They are all splendid, but the one she prefers most is of a mother and child sitting on the grass. The mother is smiling at the boy and he is laughing up at her.

"That's my father and grandmother."

Faith nearly jumps out of her skin and spins around to see Geoffrey coming towards her. Her heart is pounding aggressively and she doesn't know if it's from shock, or because she had hoped he would appear and here he is.

"Did you enjoy the evening, m'lord?"

"It was pleasant enough."

They regard each other in silence for what feels like an eternity but in reality is probably less than a minute. Suddenly, Geoffrey reaches over and grabs hold of Faith's hands.

"Marry me."

Her eyes open wide in shock.

"Before you say no, please listen. I love you. I have wanted to take care of you since the first time we met. You have found a way into my heart and my heart does not want to let you go. I know you like me for I can see it in your eyes as they light up when you see me. I am sure if you give us time you will grow to love me, even as I love you."

Tears trickle down her cheeks. This should have been the happiest day of her life.

"Please don't cry." Geoffrey leans forward and kisses her tears. She moans in a mixture of desire and distress and he crushes her in his arms, holding her tight.

"Say yes, Faith."

She wants to, oh how she wants to say yes. She longs to let him know that she loves him. She wants to make him happy and see him smile, but the image of Bertie is in her mind, so she pushes herself away from him.

Shadows from the flickering lamp on the table cast gray lights on his smooth skin but do nothing to shield the pain flooding his eyes. She can't stand it and with a sob turns and runs out of the room. She's sobbing hard by the time she reaches the stairs to the attic. She sits on the bottom one to calm herself before going up. She pulls her knees up and wraps her arms around them as she rocks to and fro and the lets the pain out. However, something curious comes over her that she won't be able to describe later on. Peace, gentle calmness and warmth within it. All a sudden, an assurance comes to her. She should tell Geoffrey everything and it will be all right. Without pausing to think where the sudden belief came from, she jumps up and races down the hallway, eager to catch Geoffrey before he retires.

Oh, please let him still be there.

As she approaches the hall she hears voices and slows down. Tiptoeing to the entrance, she stands to the side of the door and listens to Geoffrey and Margaret talking.

"You did what!"

"I love her, why shouldn't I ask her to marry me."

"You can't marry a scullery maid, what on earth are you thinking. Goodness, Geoffrey, she was a barmaid before coming to us. What would people think if you took her as your wife?"

"I really don't care what people think, and nor should you."

"Propriety is everything and well you understand this. How many doors to you in London would be closed if you made this alliance?"

"The only door that matters to me is the door to Faith's heart."

"Don't be a fool! You know very well that the coffers are virtually empty, how will you care for Driscoll once it is all gone."

"I never thought you had such a regard for money, Margaret. Remember, Timothy says that money is the root of all evil."

"Don't misquote to me, Geoffrey! You know very well that it says *the love* of money is the root of all evil. I am not saying you should love money more than all else. When it is in caring hands it can be used to good. Not only will marrying a wealthy wife bring funds back to us, but with it we can employ people to look after the house and the lands. Where would they be without the jobs that we provide? Would you let the property go to wrack and ruin and have all these people who look to us for a living go hungry? You are lord of the manor and have responsibilities, your life is not your own to do as you wish."

Gentleness comes into Margaret's voice as she crosses the distance between them to lay a delicate touch upon his arm. "I would have you happy brother, I would. I admit that this maid has a pretty face, but so do most of the women I invited here this evening to tempt you. Yet they have more than a pretty face, they have wealthy fathers who would happily supply a handsome dowry to ensure a title in return. I am sure if you gave one of them a chance and married her that you would grow to love and appreciate her. Daphnia is a very suitable match for you. I think she'd make you a splendid wife. One you could be proud to have on your arm."

Geoffrey takes Margaret's head in his hands and places a kiss on her forehead. "Miss Delaney is a lovely lady. I will admit she is both fair of face and has a pleasant manner, but she does not have my heart. Maybe you could find a rich husband and look after Driscoll yourself if it means so much to you? I would be quite happy to have a small holding and work the land myself if it meant that Faith would marry me."

"Oh, Geoffrey."

The despair in her voice carries into the hallway and suddenly, Faith has heard enough. Hitching up her skirts she rushes back to the kitchen.

Pacing the kitchen floor Faith sees her life rushing towards her, falling like pieces of a puzzle before her eyes. The picture had begun blurred but as each piece falls into place it becomes clearer. Now Faith can see what she needs to do. Too many people will be hurt if she lets Geoffrey know how much she loves him. There is nothing for it, she has to leave.

Chapter 12

'Sorrow prepares you for joy. It violently sweeps everything out of your house, so that new joy can find space to enter. It shakes the yellow leaves from the bough of your heart, so that fresh, green leaves can grow in their place. It pulls up the rotten roots, so that new roots hidden beneath have room to grow. Whatever sorrow shakes from your heart, far better things will take their place.' — Rumi

Pain crushes her mind, more severe than the pain in her aching body and battered foot, more intense than the stabbing agony gripping her lungs. After grabbing her cape from the kitchen stand she had opened the door and fled, in her haste leaving the door open, allowing the cold fingers of the night mist to penetrate the house.

The blind urge to flee has flooded her body with adrenalin, powering her to run the fastest she has ever run. Four times she stumbled on pot holes or upturned roots not visible under the swirling icy mist. Four times she picked herself up and continued the race of her life. No time to rationalize, to plan or consider. Only the pressure of escape and the need to leave Abertillery, and those she loves and fears to hurt, far behind her.

Off Driscoll estate she races, past the Six Bells Colliery, and left onto Cemetery Road.

The road is overshadowed by an oppressive canopy of oak and beech, where moonlight is forbidden to enter between heavy branches of darkest green. Here, not only is the chill of the night's bleak touch clawing at her spirit, but also the dread of stories suddenly remembered, of vindictive fairies, and murdering ghosts.

She comes to a grinding halt, her breathing labored and painful as she tries to peer through the swirls of mist. *What was that?* Movement ahead, but who would be on this little used track in the middle of the night?

Descending dread makes her limbs like lead, her breathing slows, and she freezes. There it is again, something, someone, moving through the foggy damp towards her.

Her head swings left and right. *Where can I hide?* Her legs are heavy, refusing to move, her throat dries, palms sweat. Through the stillness of dampened night, where noise normally does not travel, comes the sound of singing, fluttering through the branches of the grand old oaks. Her heartbeat is irregular and thumping, making her sway as she becomes lightheaded and faint.

He appears. So white as to be almost transparent, his attire from an era long gone by hangs as if floating on his skeleton-like body. No emotion shows on his face, yet instinctively she knows he means her harm.

Panic. One word dominates her thoughts. Run! You must know that Faith wasn't born in Abertillery and knows not the path she's on, for if she did she would retreat, even though that would mean returning to the place she is fleeing. Singing from the right draws ever closer, filling her with as much dread as the apparition in front of her.

Decision. She lunges to the left and runs, fear gripping her shoulders in its vice-like grip. Two steps, three, four, five… then she's falling. Tumbling down the tree covered ravine. High-pitched screams escape her lungs, echoing through the valley. Her body, as light and insignificant as a seeded dandelion, bounces from ground to tree to air and back to ground, as she tumbles down the sheer slope. Her soul, of its own accord, beseeches God to save her, just before her head crashes against the gnarled, impregnable trunk of an ancient oak. Splinters of crusty old bark fly in all directions. From there her body slithers, snake like, down the last of the slope, coming to stop on the valley's leaf-covered floor, lying now like a thrown away rag doll, her arms spread wide, her body twisted, legs bent. An owl hoots into the night air. Blood seeping from the wound on the back of her head drenches her flaming-red hair that lies spread around her like a demonic halo.

Chapter 13

Woken by the early morning light seeping through the curtains, Geoffrey opens his eyes and instantly feels sick. Something is wrong with Faith; he can feel it in his spirit. He dresses with speed and rushes through the house to the kitchens.

"Good morning, m'lord," chirps Cook, giving him a smile.

"Where's Faith?" His eyes search the room and not waiting for an answer he yanks the door open and steps outside to search the courtyard. Finding no one outside, he comes back in.

"I think she might be unwell, m'lord, for she hasn't come down as yet. She left the door open last night, not like Faith that. House was as cold as death this morning." She's beating eggs and doesn't seem concerned but as he looks around he spots Olwen, who is just about to enter the room, staring at him with frightened doe-like eyes.

"Where is she?"

The intensity of his stare is somewhat bothersome, and Olwen drops her gaze from his stony face and starts shaking.

Cook looks at her in surprise. "Spit it out, girl, where is she?"

"I don't know."

"She's not in your room?" asks Cook, putting down the whisk.

Olwen shakes her head. "Her bed's not been slept in."

Geoffrey runs his hands through his hair and exhales with a moan as cramps grip him, forcing him to bend almost double.

"Yer, sit down, m'lord." Cook takes his elbow, leading him to the table.

"We've got to find her. She's in trouble, I just know it."

"Olwen, run ew fast to the stables, tell them to get Reuben and the rest of the staff, and fetch 'em back yer quick."

"Yes, Cook," says Olwen making a bolt for the door.

Geoffrey sits down, putting his elbows on the table and sinking his head into his hands. "Something's wrong, Mrs Jones, I feel it in my bones."

Cook scrutinizes him, and for the first time sees that his affections for Faith are true and pure. Not that she had ever considered he might do anything dishonorable, it is just she holds Faith in high regard and is glad he isn't trifling with her affections.

Going against protocol, she pats him gently on the shoulder. "I'm sure she'll be fine. She's a goodhearted one, and I'm sure the Lord will watch over her."

Just then Reuben, Fred, Ivor and Olwen come running into the kitchen.

Geoffrey stands up and looks at them. "Rueben, do you know where she's gone?"

"No, m'lord."

"Any of you?"

They shake their heads, shocked to see Lord Driscoll so white and distressed. His concern raises their levels of worry for the young scullery maid.

"Well, she was yer well after midnight as I left her washing dishes. So she can't have gone far. To her mother's, do you think?" Cook looks at Geoffrey for his response.

"Yes, yes of course. Fred, fetch me Donatello, I will ride into town."

"Right away, m'lord." Fred tips his finger to his forehead and races outside.

"Reuben, I've seen you on a horse, you ride rather well, do you not?"

"Yes, m'lord."

"Then go after Fred, tell him to saddle a horse for you and for Ivor. The two of you head off down the two separate paths off the estate. If she's walking she can't have got far."

"Yes, m'lord."

Without changing into riding clothes or putting on a hat, Geoffrey swings himself up onto his piebald pinto. During the fast race to the butchers Geoffrey prays for Faith's safety. Once he arrives he hammers on the door whilst holding Donatello's reins in his other hand. If she isn't here, he doesn't know what he will do.

Bernard always starts work early, so it takes only moments for him to open the door. His face displays shock at seeing Lord Driscoll at this hour of the morning. Before Geoffrey can say anything, the thought that something has happened to Faith rushes to the butcher's mind.

"What's happened to her?"

"Mr Morgan, I was sincerely hoping that she would be here with you."

"What's happening?" asks Nell appearing in the doorway behind her husband.

"We can't find Faith, Mrs Morgan."

"What?" squeals Nell, grabbing hold of Bernard's arm in a vice-like grip.

"I was hoping she had come to you."

"No, no we haven't seen her since the wedding."

"Did something happen to make the croten *(lass)* run?" asks Bernard.

"No one knows, but I have this feeling... we need to find her. Is there anywhere she likes to go to be on her own, do you know?"

Bernard and Nell both shake their heads.

"Is your old home still vacant, Mrs Morgan, maybe she went there?"

"No, it was occupied the day after we left. What are we to do?" Hysteria is infiltrating Nell's voice so Bernard wraps his arm around her.

"There's nothing else to do but search. I am going to the police station now to ask them to raise the alarm." He turns around, puts his foot in the stirrup and swings himself over the horse. "I'll check in on you often until we find her." Then he's gone, breaking the law by galloping down the street towards the station.

Pitch black and silence had been her surroundings. Nothing. No thoughts, no feelings. Emptiness. Then something begins to creep towards her peaceful nothingness. At first she seeks it out, then moans and tries to withdraw but it is too late, for the thing that encroaches upon her oblivion is pain. Agony wracks through her leg and clutches her head with brutal force.

Oh Lord, don't let me die. I don't want to die. Please let Geoffrey find me.

Then she drifts back into the blackness and within her concussion all is still, no pain of heart or body, no longing for a new beginning. Nothing.

It isn't long before the whole town knows that Faith is missing and near enough the entire population of Abertillery join in the search. It's young Tim Hemms from the Six Bells way who finally puts them on the right track.

"Tell 'is nibs what ew told me, go on now," his mother says giving Tim a shove towards Lord Driscoll.

Shy and scrunching his cap in his hands, Tim begins. "Well it's like this see, I was out looking for bloody moles." His mother smacks the back of his head for cussing. "Ouch! We've only a small allotment see, and something's been eating their merry way through our cabbages."

"Come to the point, boy," snaps Geoffrey, impatient for anything that might help.

"Well I heard a scream didn't I, and I thought to myself get home quick Tim me lad, before them ghosts get you and it's you a screaming."

"Are you sure it was a scream and not an owl's screech?" asks PC Griffin.

"I might have thought that too, but there was another one and this scream had so much pain in it I feared for me life, so I ran for me bed."

"You didn't think to report screaming?" snaps Geoffrey.

"Why no, m'lord, ew see I've often heard the ghosts along Cemetery Road, and many a time over I've been derided by everyone for repeating what I heard. So no, I stopped telling people see, cos Mam said they'd lock me up if I didn't stop telling tales."

Geoffrey looks at PC Griffin who nods in understanding and the troupe of searchers begin running towards the woodland path. Amazingly, it doesn't take long to find her. Geoffrey is soon part standing, part sliding his way down the steep embankment. He's shocked when he sees her body in its awkward position and the blood, good Heavens, the amount of blood.

"Lord, please don't let her die. Please, whatever you ask of me I will do, so long as you spare her life."

Opening her eyes is hard as her lids feel heavy. The tiny bit of light entering, when she does manage to open them slightly, is enough to blind her, making her close them again swiftly.

"That's my girl, come on baby, open your eyes."

Mam?

"Faith, sweetheart, please try to wake up."

That was definitely her mother. Faith tries again, cautiously forcing her eyelids open. At first everything's blurred, and she panics, thinking she's lost her sight.

"Mam?" she croaks.

"Oh, my love, I'm here." Faith feels pressure on her hand and realizes her mother must be squeezing it.

"I can't see you, Mam." There's panic in her frail voice.

Nell starts smothering her face with kisses. "You're all right, baby, you're all right. The doctor said you might be disorientated when you first wake, but you should be fine as the effects of the morphine wear off."

Slowly, as she comes fully awake, her eyesight clears much to her relief, and she sees the haggard face of Nell, who's obviously been crying.

Looking around the pretty room she asks, "Where am I?"

"You're in one of the bedrooms at Driscoll, sweetheart. They insisted on looking after you, until you're well enough to say where you want to be."

"Well enough?"

"Don't you remember? You had a fall and banged your head something chronic. The doctor has put stitches in your head. He had to shave a bit of your hair off but luckily it's at the bottom of the back of your head so the rest of your hair will cover it, nothing to worry about."

"Fall?"

"Yes, you fell down a ravine and banged your head. What on earth were you doing out in the middle of the night, Faith, and why were you on Cemetery Road?"

Faith closes her eyes. *Cemetery Road?* Images begin to come back, the party, the proposal and then Margaret's clear disdain for her.

"Oh no, Mam, you have to get me out of here. I want to go home, take me home." Faith tries sitting up, but feeling sick drops back down onto the huge, soft feather pillow.

"I'll take you away from here as soon as you're well enough, I promise."

"You're awake, thank heavens for that," says Margaret approaching the bed. "We've been very worried about you, gave us quite the fright you did."

"I'm sorry, that was not my intention." Faith closes her eyes again, escaping the only way she can by retreating into herself.

"Why don't you go home now, Mrs Morgan? Ivor will drive you back into town and pick you up again tomorrow morning. You're exhausted, and there is Bertie to think of. He will be wondering what has happened to his mother."

Faith opens her eyes. Thankfully her ashen face is expressionless, as her thoughts are suddenly very dark.

"Will you be all right, Faith? I am tired."

Faith turns her head back towards her mother and tries to smile. "Yes, of course, Mam. You go home and get some rest. I'll be fine, look at me in the height of comfort here."

Nell gives a half-hearted smile that doesn't reach her eyes. Faith still hasn't told her why she'd tried to run away in the middle of the night. In all seriousness she is worried about leaving her daughter here.

Faith sees her hesitation. "Go on, Mam, get some rest and maybe when you come back tomorrow I'll be up and ready to go home with you?"

Nell pats her hand, giving the briefest of smiles. "See you tomorrow then." She kisses her daughter on the forehead before leaving. In truth, she's exhausted through and through.

After Nell has gone, Margaret sits on the edge of the bed. "You gave us all a dreadful fright."

"I'm sorry."

"Why did you run?"

Faith stares at her, how can she tell the lady of the manor she'd been eavesdropping?

For a moment they study each other, assessing what might be best to say and what to leave silent. Eventually, Margaret decides it is best to be forthright. "You heard us, didn't you?"

Faith nods.

"I am sorry if what you heard caused you distress. I mean no ill-will towards you."

"You just want the best for Geoffrey."

"Yes, indeed."

"I will leave tomorrow as soon as my mother returns."

Margaret can't help the small frown that comes across her delicate features.

"What is it?" asks Faith.

"There is no space for you at the butchers."

It feels like a sledgehammer of reality and betrayal. She had momentarily forgotten her mother is living at the butchers, but worse than the reminder is the fact her mother must have talked to Margaret about it. That feels like such a betrayal. Her mam, who always professed that they were above gossip and kept themselves to themselves, has told her ladyship that

Faith is effectively homeless. The shame of it brings a rose-colored tint to her very pale cheeks.

"I have a suggestion, if you are open to hear it?"

"Yes?" replies Faith.

"I have a very dear friend who lives in Presteigne. Her cook is getting old and losing her sight and is in need of help. This is a good position, you would have your own room and more pay than I can afford to give you. Mrs Howell – the cook – will teach you all you need to know so you can replace her when she can no longer work. What do you think?"

Faith's mind thinks on all the things she's been doing for Cook lately on top of her own chores. "Will I still be the scullery maid as well?"

"No. Adeline has two scullery maids amongst her staff."

Faith lifts up her hands, studying the rough scarred skin, frequently covered with blisters and often bleeding from the harshness of the soap and scrubbing brushes. "It would be good to have my soft skin back," she says quietly.

"That's settled then. I shall send word to her straight away saying as soon as you are fit for travel I will bring you to her household myself. And Faith, that won't be tomorrow. The doctor said you should probably stay in bed for a week and I shall insist you do just that. I couldn't have it on my conscience if anything were to happen to you."

Faith studies Margaret's face. Nothing but kindness and concern radiates from her eyes and manner. She nods. This is exactly what she needs. Margaret smiles, placing her hand over Faith's, which are clutching the blanket.

"Geoffrey has been pacing the corridor outside since you arrived. I think if we don't let him in to check that you are well for himself he will wear the carpet bare. If acceptable to you I will bid him come in?"

Faith blinks. Although she wants to see him badly, she's afraid of giving in and asking him to hold her. A longing to feel his arms wrapped tightly around her, protecting and shielding her from harm, fills her senses.

Resolved, she nods, she is set on a course that will remove her from his handsome features and tender ways.

Margaret watches her brother with loving concern as he approaches the bed, before leaving and pulling the door to, so it remains open only a couple of inches.

Geoffrey sits down on the chair next to the bed, soaking in the look of her, then sighing he leans back in the seat.

"I've never been so frightened in all my life as I was when I saw you lying on the ground. I thought you were dead."

They are silent for a while, regarding each other, longing to touch but both guarded, observing as from a great distance. The desire to reach over and touch his face is strong. Faith bites down on her lip, preventing herself from saying and doing what she yearns to do.

"At least tell me why you ran? Did I offend you so much? Am I so despicable to you?"

"No!" Faith tries to sit up, her hand reaching for him. No matter what must be done, she couldn't have him thinking that she loathed and despised him.

"Lie down, Faith." He half stands, encouraging her to lie back down on the huge, duck-feather pillow. When she's settled again he takes her hand in his and gently rubs his thumb absentmindedly over her skin. "Then why did you flee?"

"I didn't know what else to do."

"You make me feel like a cad, chasing you out of what has become your home."

"You mustn't think like that, you are a perfect gentleman, it is just I... I don't want to be with anyone like that. Please don't ask me to explain as I can't, but understand I am very honored that you should ask me to marry you. Why, any girl would be."

"But I don't want any girl, Faith. I want you."

Faith pulls her hand back out of his. "I'm sure when the right woman for you comes along you will be very happy together."

Geoffrey scrapes back the chair as he stands up. His fists clench tight. "Are you in cahoots with my sister?"

"No, of course not. I just wish for your happiness, that's all."

Suddenly, he leans over her, placing his hands on either side of her shoulders, his face inches away from hers. She feels his warm breath against her face and neck. His pupils fully dilate making his eyes appear almost black as they lock onto her startled gaze. Geoffrey's smoldering eyes glance at her searchingly, so deep the stare as to make her feel naked as the day she was born. Blood rushes through her body bringing heat to her cheeks, making her chest rise and fall in quick succession.

"If I wasn't a God-fearing man I would take you now and make you mine, whether you want it or not." His face lowers another inch towards her, his lips hovering over hers. Musky cologne fills her senses.

Oh take me, my love, please make me yours.

Geoffrey moves again, his lips seek her mouth as his hand slides under her head. Cradling her head, he demands and claims her kiss. For a moment of sweet bliss she responds. She can feel him trembling, and her heart aches for the sadness she's causing him. He pulls away reluctantly, keeping eye contact as he silently pleads with her to bend to his will. Shutters fall over her expression, masking love, her features now portraying nothing but indifference. He stands, defeat resonating from every pore. Perplexed, a conundrum of such depth emits the certainty that this puzzle may never be solved.

"Goodbye, my little leek-thief."

She catches her breath as he turns, and without a backwards glance, leaves the room. Left alone she stifles her anguish in the softness of the lavender-scented plump pillow.

Chapter 14

Life is an adventure. Whether exciting or stagnant depends on the path we choose. Options, decisions, results, all are submissive to our determination. Oh, and upon that thing we call fate.

For five agonizing days she had been confined to the luxurious bedroom, feeling more deprived than she ever had in the tiny one-up one-down that she had once called home. Esther, Olwen and Cook visited her daily, their friendly chatter being the only thing keeping her sane. Nell visited two more times, but once it was agreed that Faith was going to Presteigne she admitted it was too painful to keep coming, so Faith had urged her not to return. Faith had asked to see Bertie before she left, but Nell was adamant it would be no good for anyone and so Faith had waited until the night lights had been blown out before crying her pain under the bed-covers until the early hours of dawn.

Geoffrey hadn't returned to see her again, and she learnt from Olwen that he had returned to London. Despite her good intentions of taking Faith to Adeline's house herself, Margaret had caught influenza and was confined to bed.

So here she is, riding the stage coach on her own, filled with apprehension for the future and sad beyond explanation at leaving everyone she loves behind.

Considering herself helpless to the mysterious workings of the world, Faith believes she has no say in which way the wind blows her. As the carriage bumps along, she rises and falls in her seat, comparing this journey to her life. She perceives an external force driving her forward, moving her from one situation to the next. Feeling as futile as a leaf trying to be reconnected to the branch from which it has been cruelly been ripped, she believes she is helplessly adrift and abandoned to fate.

The journey she's making will take less than a day, and she's grateful there will be no overnight stay. She is, however, very relieved when they stop briefly at coaching inns to freshen up, giving the horses a rest and picking up the occasional passenger.

The ride through the Black Mountains has flown by as she stares out of the window, drinking in the enchanting scenery. She wonders what it would be like living in one of the remote farm houses she spots, lying sunk in the lush valleys like pebbles embedded in sand.

It is late afternoon when they come to rest at the Swan Inn in Hay-on-Wye.

"Short stop," cries out the driver as Faith and the two other passengers climb out of the carriage.

No time to explore the town then, thinks Faith looking longingly down the cobbled street that promises shops of interest. Not that she would buy anything, but she enjoys looking through the windows at the delights for sale. Looking at the Swan, she decides it is not somewhere she would feel comfortable in as it is obviously for the upper-classes. Its light-stone walls hold huge paned windows through which she can see an elegant dining room. No, she would not feel at ease in there.

Setting off up Church Street at a brisk pace, she decides to have a quick look around, keeping an eye on the carriage. Should the driver come back she will see him. The first shop she comes to is Hay Post Office and General Stores. She stands in front of the window admiring the many different items, homing in on one section where a pile of books are displayed. One immediately catches her eye. A pretty embossed image of flowers on the front cover of one book makes her long to touch it. *Poems* by Emily Dickinson. Oh! How she wishes she could buy it.

A lady comes out of the shop, her wicker basket over her arm brimming with goods. She gives Faith a shy smile, pulling her shawl tightly around her before hastening up the street. Out of the corner of her eye Faith spots the driver coming out of the Inn. *Already?* She runs back down the street, frightened at being left behind.

During the last part of the journey her thoughts are not only preoccupied with Bertie and Geoffrey, but also with wondering what Emily's poems are like.

The last of the daylight has faded by the time the coach pulls up outside the Royal Oak Inn. The gas street lamps offer an orange glow, although an early evening mist is swirling off the fields and seeping into the High Street, giving the place an eerie feeling, and it is this more than the cold that makes her shiver.

"Faith?"

Turning around to see who has called her name she comes face to face with an elderly man. His face is practically lost amongst a sheep-impression beard. However, the blue eyes are light and there's something about this burly, overly hairy person which she promptly takes a liking to.

"Yes?"

"Argh, good, Mrs sent me to fetch you. Come on, we've not got far to walk. Here, let me take that for you."

Faith hands over her small carpet bag. "What's your name?"

"I'm Humphrey, worked for the Carringtons nearly all my life. You're coming into a good household, lass. Yes, you are, indeed you are."

A little dash of joy rises in Faith's heart with the hope that everyone in her new employment might be as nice as Humphrey.

He walks at a brisk pace for an elderly man, and she finds herself half running to keep up with him. They leave the High Street and walk down a short lane lined with about ten houses on each side. Humphrey turns and walks under an archway into a side alley.

"Here we are," he says opening a door. "Cookie, I've fetched her for you. Here she is, safe and sound."

"Marvelous, come on over here, girl, so I can get a good look at you."

Faith crosses the kitchen to where a rather rotund lady sits in a high-backed wooden chair. "How do you do?" says Faith, offering her hand.

Cookie, instead of shaking her hand grabs hold of it with both of hers and squeezes it tightly. "Now you mustn't feel homesick lass, we'll take right good care of you here. Have you eaten supper yet?"

"No, I only took a bite to eat for lunch with me."

"Well that's good 'cause I have a mighty good chicken broth on the go. You can join us when we eat and I will introduce you to everyone. First though, Cathy here will show you to your room. Come back in when you're ready."

"That's awfully kind of you, thank you very much."

Cookie pats her hand. "You're welcome, lass."

"This way, Miss," says a young, spotty little thing whom Faith assumes is Cathy. "We're all in the attic rooms, but your room is just along the corridor so that you're close to the kitchens." Faith follows her down a narrow hallway, passing several doors, before she opens a door on the left. "Here we are, Miss, do you want me to help you unpack?"

"Oh no, not all, I will be fine. Thank you."

"Welcome, Miss." Cathy gives a nod before hurrying back down the corridors.

Faith walks over to the bed and puts her bag down before sitting on the edge of it. She can't believe how lovely the room is. Amazingly, this is to be her room! With the door left open she can hear the staff talking and laughing in the kitchen, and suddenly she is awash with a surge of emotion. If she believed in God she would surely thank Him now for the luxury of comfort and good company.

She gives herself a little shake and stands up. This is to be her new home and the quicker she settles in the better. Opening her bag she fishes out her apron. It is time to get to work, and stop the dilly-dallying of self-centred thoughts.

"'Ere, don't be thinking you'll be doing any work tonight, young lady," says Cookie, as Faith enters the kitchen. "We're all done, more or less, and there's plenty of time for you to get stuck in tomorrow. Come, sit you down here, and tell us about yourself while we finish off. You rest that foot of yours."

Shivers of disappointment run through her, because someone has noticed her limp after she's tried so hard to walk straight.

"'Ere, what's wrong with that face?" demands Cookie pointing at her.

Faith forces her cheeks upwards to create the illusion of a smile. "Nothing, I'm just a little in awe of your kindness."

"Umm, so long as I haven't offended you, mentioning your foot, an all?"

Faith blushes and is stuck for something to say.

"Ah, I see. Well you needn't mind me. I say what I think but I never think ill of anyone. Except maybe for lazy louts, don't have much time for them."

"Nor drunks," says Humphrey sitting down at the table.

"No, don't have much time for drunks," agrees Cookie.

"Nor gamblers," adds Cathy, placing bowls around the table.

"No, nor gamblers, silly people with bird-sized brains who think if they continue throwing their money away they'll end up rich, honestly such stupidity. But yes, other than that I never think badly about a person."

"Except for pickpockets," adds the other kitchen maid, adding a large loaf of bread to the array of food on the table.

"'Ere, will you lot stop? Faith will think I have nothing good to say about anyone at this rate."

Everyone is laughing as they pull out chairs and sit around the table.

The welcome into the Carrington household is like a warm embrace. Despite being homesick and missing Bertie unbearably, Faith soon settles into a new routine and is, surprisingly, happy.

Cook, or Cookie as she likes to be called, is a thorough teacher and takes great pride in passing on her family's secret recipes.

"Never got married, see," she tells Faith one day. "So I've not got any little 'uns to pass my secrets down to. Great shame, but there it is. To be honest, I've been very comfortable here. 'Tis very sad I am, that I'll have to go because of my blooming eyes. See, with your affliction my dear, you may think you are hindered in life but I tell you, you are blessed indeed 'cause that old foot of yours well, it doesn't stop you from doing anything, now does it?"

"I suppose not."

Cookie's kneading dough, thankfully a task her hands are so used to that so long as Faith weighs out the ingredients, she can still make her popular Chelsea Buns.

Faith's preparing vegetables for today's hotpot. "Why don't you stay in the house, surely that would be easier than walking home each evening?"

"I did stay in that room most of my life, but when my mother died, God bless 'er soul, she left me Rose Cottage. It's only a short distance from here and, to be truthful, although it's tiny it's my home and I've always loved it." Cookie sighs, she isn't blind yet but her vision is blurred and getting worse all the time. She knows it won't be many a month before it goes altogether. Not being able to work is something she isn't looking forward to. The main reason for moving into the cottage was so she could plan it out. She often closes her eyes and moves around touching the furniture, getting ready for the day when blackness will come upon her completely.

"Will you be joining us in church tomorrow?"

"I'm not a believer, I'm afraid."

"Really? Well that does surprise me. I know Miss Driscoll is a very religious woman. I thought she would only employ good God-fearing people."

"Just because I don't believe in God, doesn't mean I'm not good."

"Well now, I never said it did. You mustn't jump to assumptions, young lady. Every person thinks on things in a different way. I was just asking because my cottage is along Ford Street, over the bridge and on the other side of Lugg River. It's getting to be a trek to walk all the way up to Hereford Street with my eyesight going, I could do with someone to walk with me to keep me straight, so to speak. But never you mind, I'm sure someone else will take me."

Guilt easily lies on Faith's shoulders, meaning that she finds herself speaking before thinking. "Of course I'll take you. It would be lovely to accompany you. I won't go inside though; I'll just wait around for you."

"Arr, there's a love you are, thanks a ton. Come for me eight-thirty, will you? I don't like to be late."

Presteigne Baptist church was built in 1875. Its square appearance of light colored brick is different to the huge ornate churches Faith remembers from Chester, or the dark solemn looking buildings of South Wales.

As they approach the church with their arms linked, Cookie gives Faith's arm an encouraging squeeze, sending shivers down Faith's neck. A feeling of something important about to happen fills Faith and instead of being filled with dread she feels exhilarated, without knowing why. It has rained most of the night and into the early hours of the morning. Now the clouds are being blown on their way, leaving the sun to shine down, bringing a little warmth on a cold wet morning. It also creates a breath-taking rainbow that places itself perfectly over the church.

"Well, would you look at that! Here comes a cripple and a blind woman to the house of God. Do you think He's displaying His symbol of hope for us? Maybe there's a healing inside for us today?"

At the church door Cookie doesn't disengage from Faith's arm, meaning she waltzes in taking Faith along with her.

The revival hasn't reached Presteigne yet; this much is obvious to Faith the moment she enters. The people are welcoming and friendly. She feels at home with them but knows something is missing. During the two hours she attended service at Ebenezer's she had been very aware that something strange was taking place. The room had literally buzzed with electricity, excitement and expectation. The people, including the previously subdued miners, had been exuberant, throwing their arms in the air as if to reach out and touch God, raising their voices in fervent praise and prayer in a way which had made her wary of what was going on and uncomfortable as to its authenticity.

This church, however, is restrained in comparison. It somehow allows her to slip into the pew without a second thought. Comforted by a pat on the knee from Cookie she leans back in her chair and takes in her surroundings.

The first thing she notices is the lack of people. At Ebenezer's she had to push her way through the throng of people to get a position on the balcony. Yet here, not a single person sits upstairs, there are ample places to sit in the pews downstairs. She studies the huge organ pipes and a warm feeling spreads through her body as someone begins to play. She stands when everyone else does and when they start singing she joins in. It feels right and even though strange emotions move within her spirit and tears trickle down her cheeks, she knows suddenly that she needs to know more about this God that so many people worship.

The next two weeks fly by and it is only when she is on her own at night does Faith allow her sorrow out and cry into her pillow. During the day she is kept busy by Cookie who is determined to turn her into a master of the kitchen stove. She had also taken it upon herself to share her beliefs and to fill each day with stories from the Bible.

Fascinated by the stories Faith becomes hungry for more and more, bombarding her with questions all day long.

"Why do you think God put the Song of Solomon into the Bible?"

"Ah. Now, we may *think* the world has fallen more wicked by the day, and that we are in a place which has never been *so* evil as it is now but... in truth it is not so. From the moment the apple was eaten sin entered and has remained with us, but it has not changed, oh no. No amount of preaching that we fall deeper in sin is accurate. There is only light and dark. Gray is an illusion which lets the dark pretend it is not so. I believe Solomon wrote the song of love as he was desperate to reach back to a time of innocence. A time when love was pure and open, and not something to be covered. Some believe coming together in that intimate union is a thing for procreation only, 'tch! I say to that. God is love. It is who He is, and He made us in His image so that we may love and be loved. There is no point to life without love."

Crimson flushes bring heat to Faith's face as she turns her back on Cookie and starts beating the cake mixture with extreme gusto. What had transpired between herself and Harrison hadn't felt either good or love. It had felt like sin, bringing with it a self-condemnation that continues to crush her soul. Yet without that moment she would never have had Bertie, and he is her joy, her love. She is lost to the utter belief that she's wicked through and through. There will never be any returning to innocence for her.

With a dampener on the day, Faith finds herself locked in her own thoughts. Cookie, instinctively knowing something's wrong, offers a loving arm and a listening ear. Faith turns her down. She's already shared her dark secret with one person, and she can't bring herself to do so a second time, no matter how lovely Cookie is.

Chapter 15

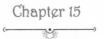

Hope is the thing with feathers -
That perches in the soul

Unable to sleep, Adeline rises early, getting dressed without assistance. She sweeps her long auburn hair up and pins it in a soft bun on the back of her head. Normally a good sleeper, she is puzzled by how alert and awake she feels. In slippered feet she floats down the stairs feeling a buzz of mystery in the air. Turning a corner, she catches sight of two maids whispering in the corridor. They stop as soon as they see her, but appear too guilty for her to let it pass.

"Only scoundrels and reprobates hide their words behind hands and silent sniggers, out with it girls, what malice are you stirring up?"

They curtsy, stuttering their responses, both babbling at the same time. "Oh no, milady we're not up to no mischief. It's Faith, we're right worried about her we are."

"What's wrong with the girl?"

"Well, we don't rightly know, but she does cry every night she does, and it sounds so pitiful it near breaks our hearts."

Taking in their candid expressions, she decides to believe them. "You should know that I do not tolerate any spreading of tales in this household."

Both girls nod and confirm their agreement several times.

"That being said, I can see you are sincere, so go about your work."

They curtsy before hurrying down the corridor.

Adeline prides herself in running a happy home. One which reflects the love she and her husband have, not only for each other, but also for the Lord. It hurts to think that the cook's new assistant is unhappy. She goes to the wall and pulls the rope that makes a bell ring in the kitchen. Within moments there's a gentle knock on the door.

"Come in."

The door opens and Cookie appears. "You rang for me, milady?"

"Close the door, Cookie, and come and sit down with me."

Nervous and fearing she has done something wrong Cookie sits, fidgeting with her fingers, waiting for Lady Carrington to speak.

"It has been brought to my attention that our new girl is rather unhappy, do you know what might be causing this?"

Cookie's shoulders droop in relief. "No, milady, she's not confided in me."

"You have no clue?"

"Well, besides her foot, which she tries her hardest to hide but I know causes her discomfort, I think she's missing her family."

"Do you believe this is what causes her to cry each night?"

Cookie looks straight at Adeline. She has worked for her Ladyship for many years and knows her to be fair and just, a person you can rely upon. Still, talking about Faith when she isn't present feels a little like betrayal. "I think the Lord is calling to her, yet she resists. I have the impression she believes she's not worthy to receive His love."

"I've noticed the sorrow in her eyes. I had hoped we might take it away from her. Shall we try, Cookie, what do you say?"

"It may only be possible with God's help."

Adeline stands up and starts pacing. After a moment she stops and clicks her fingers in the air. "I've got it, we're going to take a trip to Loughor, and what's more we're going today."

"*We* are?"

"Yes, we are, the three of us are going to go and see Evan Roberts. And if God is good, and we know He is, then He will use this young man to reach our new addition to the household and restore to her some joy!"

Precisely one hour later, Adeline, Cookie and Faith sit in the coach and set off for South Wales. The first week of December, with its oppressive ashen skies, threatened snow but, as yet, the cold flakes remain tightly within its cloudy grasp. The wind is biting and Faith is glad for the extra blankets Lady Carrington had them bring. In her sudden haste to reach the man of revival Adeline hadn't thought too much on how long it would take them to get there. She is, therefore, grateful that she called for a four horse carriage. If the driver sets them at a steady pace they should be there by nightfall.

"My sister lives in Swansea, so we shall spend the night with her and then go on to Loughor in the morning."

Faith asked no questions when told to wrap up for a journey but now, in the carriage, she is burning to know why they are racing down Wales like escapee prisoners. Adeline, however, who suffers from carriage sickness, is disinclined to talk so keeps her eyes closed most of the time, thus discouraging Cookie and Faith from talking too much.

It makes the day long, being cooped up with nothing but her thoughts, and dwelling on her failings doesn't help Faith's spirits either. She is extremely relieved when close to midnight they arrive outside a tall seafront house. Cookie and Faith are shown to a tiny attic room where they have to share a small bed and so will sleep top-to-tail. Faith tries asking Cookie why they are there but she just grunts a reply, saying she is exhausted and needs a proper sleep.

Faith is surprised to find they slept well past eight a.m. without anyone coming to wake them.

"I guess milady asked for us to be left to ourselves this morning," says Cookie. "Very considerate of her. She knows my arthritis is triggered by the damp air."

They find their way down to the kitchen where they're given some heated oats and a pot of tea, much to Cookie's pleasure. They have only just finished eating when a maid approaches them.

"Lady Carrington has asked that you be ready to leave shortly. There is a revival meeting today in Loughor Chapel, and she wants to be sure to arrive in time to get a seat." Thanking her they quickly finish the tea before going back to the room to fetch their capes and bags.

"And you are sure they are fine to carry on today?"

"Yes, milady. They are rested and ready to go," replies the driver.

"Good, ah, here come my companions for the day."

Cookie and Faith join Adeline on the sea-front road. The sea-breeze whisking around their faces is biting cold and salty. They hasten inside the carriage to shelter from the barrage of damp wind.

The journey to Loughor only takes them an hour. Faith is disappointed when they lose sight of the sea, but is cheered again when they come to their destination, finding they are once again near the coast.

"The sea's a lot calmer here," she says as they climb out of the carriage.

"That's not the sea, Miss," says the driver. "That's the River Loughor."

"Oh."

"Mr Green, are you sure you have brought us to the correct place? I can't see a church here. We are in Glebe Road?"

"Yes, milady, but I believe it is a long road and we're at one end of it. I think it might be best if you return to the carriage, and I will proceed slowly."

"Very well."

They travel along the road for ten minutes before the church is spotted. Not by its impressive brickwork, but by the queues of people waiting to enter.

"Shall I wait with the driver, milady?" asks Faith hoping the answer will be yes.

"No, come along and take Cookie's arm, so she feels safe in the crowd."

"Thank you, my dear," says Cookie as Faith slips her arm through hers.

It's hard to believe there's still two hours to go before the service starts. The crowd of people waiting to get in huddle together in their coats and capes, trying to avoid the biting wind with their fellow attendee's body.

They join the queue and Faith looks at Adeline in shock. "Won't you wait in the carriage, milady? I will come and fetch you once we have gained access and got seats."

Adeline smiles, and reaching up with her gloved hand touches Faith's face. "We are all the same in the house of God, but thank you for the offer."

Luckily, they don't have long to wait before the doors open and the crowd begins piling in.

Most of the ushers are crying out instructions in Welsh, but as they approach one calls out in English, "Any infirm, come this way."

"Young man, Mrs Howell here is practically blind, and Faith has a club foot."

Faith's face burns as shame surges through her at having someone's attention brought to her deformity.

"Then please enter through the center doors and take a seat as near to the front as possible." Having given his instructions he turns back to face the crowd again. "All able-bodied people to the side doors please, for balcony seating."

The three ladies are swept along by the urgency of those around them, and soon find themselves sitting in a pew only five rows back from the pulpit. Excited chatter fills the church with a humming buzz. Faith finds herself trying to shrink back into her seat, wishing to be invisible. Adeline and Cookie chat away like old friends, holding hands in their expectant demeanor. It isn't long before they hear a disappointed cry from the crowd outside as it is announced the church is full and can hold no more.

"You all right, me dear?" asks Cookie.

Faith nods.

As soon as the doors are closed a signal is given to start the proceedings of the meeting, even though it is hours before its advertised time. An animated whisper spreads throughout the congregation.

"Look, it's the Davies sisters and Miss Jones."

Three young women walk to the front of the platform. By the time they're standing still, an expectant hush has flooded the church. Miss Annie Davies takes one step in front of the other two ladies. Not waiting for the organ she begins to sing, 'Dyma yw Cariad' *(Here is love)*. From the first note shivers ripple over Faith's entire body. The hairs on her arms stand on end as she realizes she is in the presence of something extraordinary. She has heard 'Here is Love' many times in the last year, in both English and Welsh, but has never experienced the power of the words as she does now. By the end of the first chorus the organ has crept in, almost unnoticed. As the other ladies take up the song, Faith is done for. Openly sobbing, she can do nothing to stay the tide of emotions being released. Even though she is crying herself, Cookie manages to shove a handkerchief into Faith's hands.

All around them people wail and cry with unashamed abandon, or lift their arms to heaven and sing with all their heart. After four songs the three ladies go to the side of the church and sit down in chairs placed there for them.

As if in a hurry, a tall, gaunt-looking man with curly fair hair strides with gracefulness across the floor. He stops in front of the pulpit. Standing there in a long, double-breasted coat, there isn't much about him to show he is a man of worthy note. Faith had heard that in his early years he worked down the mine alongside his father, and that it was only in recent times he had earnestly sought God and become a minister. He looks younger than his twenty-seven years and in no way does he impress upon her that he's anything other than an ordinary man.

"Is God with you?" Evan Roberts asks the congregation.

The people erupt with their replies. "Yes, He is."

"Are you sure?"

The response is rapturous as they confirm their belief that God is indeed with them.

"Good, then you don't need me." He turns to leave and shocks of dismay are heard in a thousand gasps.

"Before you go, tell me, can so great a sinner as I be saved?"

There's an explosion of whispers, for the woman who has stood to address Evan Roberts is none other than the young woman who had recently been a prominent figure in a police-court case, a female of much ill-repute.

Evan stops in his tracks and turns to look at her. "Yes, certainly. There is no sinner too great who cannot be saved."

Hearing his response the young woman seems to pass into an ecstasy of joy and with tears falling down her cheeks she cries aloud, "I have fallen as low as anyone, and He has saved me. Come to Him, one and all."

What follows is simply indescribable. Most of the densely crowded gathering are standing and shouting, 'Amen' and 'Diolch byth' *(thank goodness)*. Many people start weeping.

Evan raises his arms and starts praying. A measure of stillness returns to the people as his eyes roam through the crowds, both in the pews before him and on the balcony above. When his eyes fall upon Faith and stay there she feels like a rabbit caught by the lamp and is frozen with fear. Releasing her gaze at last he looks up, and Faith sighs with relief. Her body is trembling so much that the pew moves beneath her.

"Bend us oh Duw, bend us to thy will," Evan prays.

Amens in both English and Welsh rush through the pews.

"Confess your sins to Duw, and put away any wrong done to others. Put away any doubtful habits. Obey the Holy Spirit promptly, and confess that Christ is the Lord, openly and unashamedly. These four things will lead to you receiving the light and the presence of God in your life."

Many people instantly start praying aloud for God to forgive them, and Faith has a stirring inside her like never before. She crushes the words that rise in her throat, forbidding them to exit.

Evan approaches one of the women on the stage, giving her some instruction before leaving.

Sarah Jones, the woman Evan spoke to, preaches to them then, earnestly beseeching all to welcome the Lord into their lives. A man gets up from a front seat to say he has noticed that there were 100,000 applicants every year for enlistment in the Army "of our noble King Edward." But of those, sixty-two percent were declared unfit for enlistment. Whereas, during the last few months, through the revival, no less than 80,000 had applied for enlistment in the army of King Jesus, and not one was regarded as unfit. All; the maimed, the lame, the blind, all who had a soul to save, were welcomed.

Miss S.A. Jones, taking the cue from this, makes an eloquent appeal for everyone to join God's army, and instead of taking the King's shilling they would be given a heavenly crown. Many people flood to the front of church to bow and profess their new-found faith in Jesus. Faith resists the urge to join them. Her imprisonment to self-loathing is too strong a cage to break out of herself. She might have remained a prisoner to it her entire life, except that God has other plans for her.

"Aghh!" Cookie's scream terrifies Faith and she turns, seeking what has caused Mrs Howell so much pain.

"I can see! I can see!" Cookie leaps up and starts jumping up and down. "I can see, clear as a bell I tell 'ee. I can see!"

Hallelujah, Amen and Canmol Duw *(praise God)* floods the church. Adeline starts jumping up and down with Cookie, while Faith collapses in a heap on the floor.

At first, Faith isn't sure where she is and is too frightened to try to sit up.

"Hush, there. Take your time, there is no rush."

With her sight slowly coming into focus she gazes up into the beautiful face of Miss Sarah Jones. Immediately, a feeling of peace falls upon her spirit.

With a soft smile which floods her eyes with caring love, and with hair that looks like a halo, Sarah offers Faith a hand and helps her to stand up.

"Let's sit here for a while," says Sarah taking hold of Faith's hand, leading her towards two chairs.

"Where are we?"

"We're in the old building next door to the church. You mustn't worry. The women you came with know where you are and won't leave until you're ready."

"I must go, I can't keep them waiting." Faith tries to stand.

Sarah pulls her back down into the chair. "They are worshiping next door, trust me, they are in no rush to leave. Your friend Mrs Howell has had a miraculous healing. I think she would worship all night long if she could."

"Her sight really came back?"

"Yes, she says she can see nits jumping in children's hair, her sight is that good. Now, my dear, tell me, why do you resist the love of God?"

Emotionally exhausted from all the crying Faith lets her grief pour out, spilling her entire life-story. All her thoughts and assumptions pour out to this complete stranger. Sarah doesn't interrupt, simply listens, giving the occasional nod. Faith is reassured by the woman's sympathetic and understanding manner.

"So now you see why God would not want me," she finishes.

"Do you know I was a useless, giddy, frivolous girl? Oh, very frivolous. Then one day I listened to Evan preaching and my life changed completely. I know I will never be the same. You see, the moment we give our life to Christ, our old self dies and is no more. We are new creations who have chosen to walk a new path."

"But…"

"There are no buts, *all* who call on the name of Jesus will be saved, and if you confess your sin, He is just and swift to forgive."

"How then, how can He love me?"

"Because He is love, it is His very nature. Why don't you give Him a chance, Faith? What have you to lose?"

"I couldn't cope with being rejected again." Faith buries her face in her hands, trying to hide from her past pains.

Sarah strokes her head. "Trust me, Faith, God will never, ever, reject you. Come, put your hands down and say a prayer with me. Let today be the first day of the rest of your life. Be reborn and filled with the Spirit."

There and then, Faith repeats the prayer after Sarah. When she whispers amen at the end she half expects some supernatural event to take place, but nothing happens, except for a feeling of complete peace and well-being.

"Now, about Geoffrey," says Sarah, tilting Faith's chin up with her finger.

Faith looks back at her with hope-filled, questioning eyes.

"Do you know the story of Gideon?"

Faith shakes her head.

"Gideon was a man after God's own heart, and even though he was a poor farmer, God gave him a huge task. Wanting to be sure that he had really heard God talk to him, Gideon asked God to perform a small miracle and to keep the land dry whilst the fleece would collect the dew. God answered the request, which is why today some people lay down their own fleece before Him, and ask for it to be a sign from Him so they know what they are doing is right in His eyes. This is what I want you to do. Close your eyes."

Faith closes her eyes.

"Now empty your mind of everything if you can, for I am going to ask you a question which will bring something to your mind. What comes, do not speak out but keep between you and God. Nod if you understand."

Faith nods.

"I want you to think of something that you would like to have, something quite small, but something that no one in the world knows that you want."

Immediately the image of the book of poems she had seen in Hay-on-Wye comes into her mind.

"Do you have something?"

Faith nods.

"Now pray after me…" Sarah's grip on Faith's hands increases.

"Dear Lord, please give this thing as a gift to me so I may know that Geoffrey and I should be together. And if this thing should not materialize then I know that I should remain in Presteigne and put him from my mind. Amen."

When she utters the word amen Faith's eyes fly open, and she searches Sarah's face. "Do you think God might really answer this prayer?"

"I sincerely do."

Chapter 16

Much joy floods both the Carrington's household and the neighborhood when Mrs Howell returns home with perfect vision.

It is just as well, as Christmas time is approaching and the whole town becomes up in arms ready to celebrate this wonderful gift from God.

"It is a week earlier than normal, but I would like us to decorate the house," announces Adeline to her staff. "I feel the joy of the Lord in my bones and I need to rejoice. What better way than remembering the day our Lord Jesus came down to earth to save us."

There is a constant flood of people to the back door asking if Cookie might pray with them. With Faith there to shoulder a lot of the work, Lady Carrington gives her consent for these visits to continue.

Faith loses count of the number of times people look upon her in compassion and mumble 'your blessing will come, dear.' In truth, she thanks them with all sincerity as she is indeed waiting for her blessing, although not as they might think. The healing of her foot no longer bothers her. What has become the most precious wish within her heart is that a certain book should somehow, miraculously, arrive in her hands.

Adeline receives numerous visitors herself as news of her servant's healing spreads throughout the gentry. She welcomes them all, even the skeptics, with a warm smile, a pot of tea and a tray of cakes. Mr Carrington kissed his wife's forehead and gave his approval for her constant stream of visitors and then promptly retired to his study where peace and quiet reign.

Cookie is often called to the parlor to tell the tale of her healing. Adeline is overjoyed when friends she has tried to reach for years ask to be led in the prayer of salvation. And so, without the man himself visiting Presteigne, Evan Robert's revival fire came to town.

Faith is invited to many prayer meetings but declines as she is still finding her feet in regards to being able to talk to God herself. Lacking confidence to pray in public, she whispers to God in the sanctuary of her own room. Oh, and whisper she does! She finds herself surprisingly drawn to talk to God all day long, inside her head, of course. At night she kneels by her bed and speaks out loud – just in case it is easier for God to hear her.

After a week has passed the knocks to the back door die down somewhat. Finally, the Carrington household is left to get on with their preparations for Christmas celebrations. Today they're making mincemeat, steeped in brandy, and bottling it ready for mincemeat pies.

With the howling wind and the crackling wood on the fire it takes three knocks on the door before Faith realizes someone is outside. Wiping her hands on her apron she hastens to the door and lifts the heavy latch. She's greeted by the post man, who is barely visible under all his scarfs, hat and huge coat.

"Thank heavens for that," he says shoving a parcel at Faith. "I was just about to leave." He tips his hand to his hat, turns and hurries back down the street.

"What is it?" asks Cookie.

"It's a parcel for me," answers Faith in obvious surprise. She goes to the table and puts the small parcel down. A sudden excitement floods her as she studies the package.

It is wrapped in brown paper and tied with string. Like any parcel it is plain and ordinary, however, she doesn't recognize the writing. Her mother is the only person who has written her a letter up to now. With shaking fingers she uses the knife to cut the string, and then carefully folds back the paper. Before her lies the book she'd seen in the shop window in Hay-on-Wye. The beautiful soft brown leather, embossed with gold writing which simply says, 'Poems' Emily Dickinson.

She squeals, throwing her arms in the air, nearly exploding with joy.

"Let me see," says Cookie, wiping her hands on the towel and coming over. "My, that's a pretty book. I didn't know you liked poems."

Faith, however, is speechless. When Cookie finishes inspecting the book and hands it back, Faith takes it and runs to her room.

"That's strange indeed, that is," mutters Cookie as she goes back to labeling jars.

In her room Faith sits on the bed and looks at the book in shock. *How can this be? Can God really have sent it to me to tell me I should be with Geoffrey?*

As she opens the book a slip of paper and a pressed carnation fall out. She picks them up and even though she knows the dried flower will have no smell she sniffs it anyway. Geoffrey knows that carnations are her favorite flower. She reads the note.

> *Faith,*
> *I know I must let you go, but before I do please accept this gift from me. It is a small thing that I give you in exchange of my heart, as my love you will not accept. I will stop now, and desist in my yearnings for your love. And so I say goodbye.*
> *Geoffrey.*

Oh no! How can this be? What cruel trick is this that she should receive the very thing she asked God for, only to learn that Geoffrey has finally given up on her? She can't cry. She's so confused. Then from the corner of her eye she notices that one of the pages has been bent. She opens the book at that page and reads the poem upon it.

> *Hope is the thing with feathers -*
> *That perches in the soul -*
> *And sings the tune without the words -*
> *And never stops - at all -*
>
> *And sweetest - in the Gale - is heard -*
> *And sore must be the storm -*
> *That could abash the little Bird*
> *That kept so many warm -*
>
> *I've heard it in the chillest land -*
> *And on the strangest Sea -*
> *Yet - never - in Extremity,*
> *It asked a crumb - of me.*

What did it mean, and what was Geoffrey trying to tell her? Was God telling her something? Should hope remain in her soul? Was asking God for a sign like asking for a crumb? She didn't understand. If God was playing a trick it was the worst thing in the world He could have done to her. And what of Geoffrey? Why send her such a beautiful gift and in it say goodbye?

She returns to the kitchen subdued and pale. Cookie takes one look at her and puts the kettle on the hook over the fire, to make some tea.

"Make the pastry for the Beef Wellington, will you dear."

Faith fetches flour, butter and lard and sets about making the covering for the beef.

"Keep the touch light, or you'll make the pastry tough."

When the water is ready, Cookie pours it into a teapot. "Now, when that's a brewing, why don't you tell me what's wrong?"

Faith tells her about how Miss Sarah Jones had suggested she lay a fleece before God. "Do you think it was wrong of me to ask God to help me with matters of the heart?"

"No child, of course not. The Lord is concerned with everything about us and He loves to give us the delights of our hearts. That's what the Bible says, so of course He is concerned when we are in love and yet sad."

"Still, Geoffrey has sent the book I asked only God for, no one else knew I liked the book so much, no one. Yet, here he tells me he has put his love for me out of his heart. I don't understand."

"Tell me, child, do you love yourself?"

"Heavens no, I am a terrible person."

"And therein, I believe, is the root of your conundrum, for if you do not love yourself you will never believe that anyone else could love you."

"My mam and Bertie love me."

"Do you really believe that?"

Right away, Faith's mind recalls the thoughts which make her cry so hard at night. Her mother has happily moved in with Bernard, even when there isn't space for Faith to live there. As for Bertie, he is certainly more taken with Eva at the moment and has settled into his new family with apparent ease. Her chin trembles and her throat constricts as a well of emotion begins to overtake her.

"Tell me your thoughts."

A barrage of built up emotions pour from Faith as Cookie sits quietly and listens. "They might have loved me once, but they soon moved on without me so their love couldn't have been real."

"Now you listen to me." Cookie grabs both of Faith's hands and squeezes them tightly. "I've only known you for the shortest of times, but I have come to love you. I can see that your mam did a wonderful thing raising you otherwise you wouldn't be who you are today. No person could accomplish that unless love ran deep through their veins. These thoughts of rejection that bombard you and give you no peace, they are of darkness and you must let them go. Do you hear me?"

Sniffing, Faith nods.

"You need to understand that God created you the way you, *exactly* the way you are, and He loves you unconditionally. For you to think you are unworthy of love is to make out that God doesn't know what He's doing. Don't you think I questioned Him more than a little on why I was going blind? Oh, right distressed I were, when I realized it wasn't a passing illness and that my semi-blindness was permanent and getting worse. I ranted and raved at Him good and proper, full blast from my lungs He did get."

Faith looks at her with a light in her eyes, she can well imagine Cookie blasting her anger. "Did God answer you?"

"He did indeed."

"You heard him?" Faith is filled with awe.

"Not His voice, but His spirit. Like a gentle whisper I felt I heard proverbs in my mind, so I went straight to the Bible and opened it to proverbs, and there before me was… trust in the Lord with all your heart, and lean not on your understandings. And whoosh, just like that all my distress was taken away from me and I was filled with peace."

"That is lovely."

"God loves you, Faith, I love you, and I am sure your mother loves you more than life. So if this Geoffrey of yours has declared his love to you and even asked you to marry him, how can you entertain for even a moment that he no longer loves you?"

"But his letter…"

"Was written because he's hurting, and he's trying to give you what you want."

"So you think he loves me still?"

"I don't know him, but if his love is true and from all you have told me I believe it must be so, then love does not die simply because we have put pen to paper. So what are you going to do?"

"My holiday starts the day after Boxing day, so I will go and tell him I have changed my mind!"

"Now there's the spirit! Come on, let's get this beef in the oven."

The days leading up to Christmas Eve are a pure joy and the household is full of laughter and singing. Lord Carrington is an accomplished pianist and in good nature allowed his wife to bully him into playing whenever he isn't working in his study. Adeline and her friends lift their voices singing carols, then sip hot mulled wine and exchange presents to put under the tree. The staff, if in earshot, join in the singing and even old Humphrey, not a supporter of Yule-tide celebrations (for reasons he refuses to disclose), found he could

166

resist not and joins in when the staff sing around the kitchen as he warms his boots by the fire.

"I can't believe tomorrow is Christmas Eve," says Faith, popping yet another batch of pies into the oven.

"Not long now and you'll be able to set off for home and visit your family." Cookie is happy to see the sparkle in Faith's eyes, not only because she can see it so clearly, but also because it shows the girl's happiness brimming over.

"You'll be all right when I've gone?"

"Eee lass, Cookie here was managing the kitchen well before you came, 'tis sure to manage for seven days when you're gone!"

Faith gives Humphrey a gentle nudge in the arm. "I hope she doesn't manage too well without me or Lady Carrington might not want me back."

"Maybe… you might not *want* to come back." She gives Faith a knowing look which causes Faith to blush.

"'Ere what's going on, you're not leaving us already are you?" asks Humphrey, leaning forward in his chair.

"Now never you mind, old man. What will be, will be and you'll just have to wait and see."

"Huh, you women are not straightforward, nope never a clear word so we poor men might understand. Air of mystery you like and 'tis in riddles you do talk, huh! Think I'll take myself off to the inn, in need of a drink I am now."

"Go on with you, you're always in need of a drink, don't have anything to do with our conversation," chuckles Cookie.

Just then the kitchen bell on the far left rings. "Too late, Humphrey, looks like Lady Carrington wants you."

"Won't you go, Cookie? Tell her I had to go fetch something for you." Humphrey looks comical in his pleading stance, hands clasped and eyebrows raised in hopeful expectation.

"I'll go up for you," says Faith.

"And what if the mistress wants coal shifting upstairs, you going to do that for the lazy so and so?"

"I don't mind."

"Bless you, lass." Before Cookie can argue, Humphrey shoots out of the back door, grabbing his coat as he goes.

Faith washes her hands and puts on a clean apron before rushing up the stairs to the parlor.

"Ah, Faith. Is Humphrey not available? I thought he was back from the butchers?"

"He just popped out for something for Cookie, milady, I'm sure he will return soon."

"Oh, that is bad timing, I need him to go to the post office for me. He could have done the two things at the same time. Will you take this for me? It is a congratulations message to be telegrammed to Lord Driscoll, it really needs to go today."

"Yes, of course, milady. I'll go right away."

"Tell the postmaster to put it on my account, please," says Adeline handing over an envelope.

"Yes, milady." Faith bobs a quick curtsy and turns to leave.

"I have to go to the post office. I'll be back as quick as I can." Faith takes her cape off the stand and swings it around her shoulders before lifting the hood over her head.

"Here, lass, take my gloves because it's mighty cold out there. That North wind has been blowing a while now, snow is on the way and that's the truth."

"Thank you. Hopefully I won't be in it long enough to get too cold." Faith slips her hands into the gloves that are too big for her, but will definitely keep her warm.

It isn't until she is rushing up the high street, pushing against the biting wind that Adeline's words sink in. *Congratulations to Lord Driscoll, I wonder what has happened?*

She's grateful when she reaches the post office, although shutting the door behind her turns out to be a battle as the wind is blowing full pelt against it.

"I have a telegram to be sent for Lady Carrington please, to be put on her account." Faith hands the small envelope over the counter to the postmaster.

"No problem. I'll do it now so wait, and when it's gone you will be able to report back to Lady Carrington that it was well sent." The postmaster begins opening the letter and Faith finds her eyes glued on it, hoping to catch its contents. She needn't have worried for as the postmaster taps away at his Morse code he reads the message aloud.

"Congratulations. On. Your. Planned. Engagement. Geoffrey. Daphnia. Is. A. Lucky. Lady. See. You. In. The. New. Year. Best. Wishes. Richard. And. Adeline."

The postmaster puts the letter back in the envelope and passes it back to Faith. "You tell her ladyship that it went and has been received."

Faith doesn't move. She stares with unseeing eyes into the puzzled face of the postmaster. "Miss?"

She puts out her hand and takes the envelope. Without speaking, she turns around and walks out of the shop. She walks to the end of the road where she should turn left to go back to the Carringtons. But her feet will take her in that direction no further. She stands as the wind whips her cape and makes it flutter in the air. Her mind is blank. In fact, very few thoughts can penetrate her state of shock. Her feet take over and she starts walking out of town.

Moving quickly, she soon finds herself out of Presteigne, and on the coach-road heading south. Almost an hour has passed before she hears something approaching behind her. In sudden hope of catching a lift, she stops and starts waving. The farmer pulls on his horse's reins, drawing the cart to a stop beside her.

"This isn't the weather for a walk, Miss. What you doing out here?"

Faith looks at the letter briefly and then holds it up. "I have just received news from home. I must get back straight away. Will you take me a ways with you?"

"Sorry to hear that, lass. Where you heading then?"

"Abertillery." She looks at the burly farmer and her heartbeat quickens as she hopes he might be going all the way.

"Ooow, that's a fair grand way you have to go. I will be able to take you about half-way as I go down as far as Pengenffordd, but I won't be able to take you any further. You'll have to wait there for the Cardiff coach, but tell you the truth I do, I don't even know if the coach is running today. Wouldn't you be better to go back and wait until the Christmas season has passed when the coach will be definitely running again?"

"I can't wait. It's an emergency. I must get home as soon as possible. I am very grateful for your offer to take me as far as Pengenffordd, thank you so much."

"Come on then, climb on up. Got to warn you though, it's not warm up here."

She steps up onto the wheel and uses it to climb up next to the farmer.

Luckily for Faith, who is still frozen in her shock, the farmer isn't a talker. Besides, with the wind howling around them talking would have been difficult. From the small bit of conversation they do manage at the beginning he tells her his name is Henry, and that he has just delivered a pile of firewood to Presteigne. He is now returning home, and as the cart isn't full they will make good time.

They have only been traveling for about two hours when it starts to snow. Henry reaches under the seat and pulls out a hessian sack, shoving it at her. "Wrap this round your shoulders. It will help keep you dry. Proper good stuff it is, go on now."

Faith unfolds the large cloth and wraps it around her. "Thank you."

"Let's get home to Pengenffordd before the clouds dump the lot on us."

Faith holds the cloth tightly around her. With her hood covering her lush red hair, and the hessian pulled up to cover her frozen nose, only her deep brown eyes are visible.

"You look like a gypsy you do."

She almost smiles back at him but turns her attention back to the ever whitening scenery around them. Shock is wearing off now, and she is a mass of distressful thoughts. The thought which upsets her most is that Cookie and Lady Carrington will be worried when she doesn't return and she has no means of telling them where she is. Shame stemming from her thoughtless actions is enough to heat her through the cold.

The other thought that makes her swoon with sickness is that Geoffrey is going to marry someone else. *How can he, when he so recently declared his love for me?* She has to get to him, she needs to tell him that she loves him, and more than a secret flame inside her it is the love that a woman gives to her husband. Freely, unconditionally and abundantly. No, she can't let him propose to someone before he knows that she will marry him. *If he still wants me?*

The snowflakes are large and fluffy and it isn't long before the dark browns of winter leave, masking the trees and fields in pure white. *It's so beautiful.* Though the tree trunks and larger branches remain almost black, the smaller branches become white and carriers of wool-like clusters. She is glad Henry knows where he's going because the track has become smaller as it merges with the fields.

She's so frozen she can't feel her toes or fingers when Henry finally pulls the cart to a stop in front of an Inn called the Dragon's Back.

"If the coach is coming today it will stop here briefly, but I'm afraid this is as far as I can take you. I have to get the sheep gathered up before the storm really breaks."

"You think it is going to snow even more than this?"

"'Tis a North wind see, and I can feel it in my bones that it's bringing a right storm with it. It has been building in power all day and before night fall it will release the tide of it, and that's the truth."

Climbing down is slow work, as her limbs are too stiff to move with ease. "Thank you, you have been very kind to bring me this far."

"Listen here, and mark me well, girl. If the coach doesn't come this afternoon, you kip down with Sally. She's a good 'un and she'll only charge you a bob or two."

Faith's face must have revealed her sudden thought of horror as to the fact she doesn't have any money on her.

"Don't tell me you left without your purse!"

"I wasn't thinking anything except for the need to get home. I will be all right, don't worry about me. I am sure I can get another lift a bit further down the road."

Henry jumps down and grabs her by the arm, then marches her into the Inn. "Sally?"

"Hello, lovie, who you got there?" A fat woman wobbles out from behind the bar.

"Here's thruppence, give her a bowl of soup, will you?"

"Sure thing," says Sally pocketing the money.

"And this," he takes hold of her hand and places some copper in it, "this is to pay for the coach."

"I, I, I don't know what to say."

"Listen, lass, my daughter's about your age and I'd like to think someone would look after her if she were in need. So you just take it, and whenever you get a chance then pass the blessing on to someone else."

"I will. Thank you so much."

"But you mark my words. If that coach doesn't turn up, you make sure you don't get no lift from anyone else. You don't know what kind of ruffian you might be handing yourself over to. Do you understand?"

Faith nods. If she doesn't actually agree out loud she wouldn't be breaking her word, now would she?

"Angel heart that man has," says Sally as Henry leaves. "Now let's get you a bowl of soup."

Chapter 17

Faith is being sure of what we hope for
& certain of what we do not see
Hebrews 11:1

A swirl of biting wind rushes through the room as the only other patron leaves the inn. Sitting by the fire in the Dragon's Back she is practically on her own, as Sally is now well-drunk and lying slumped on a couch at the back of the room. Watching the flickering flames dance in the hearth Faith contemplates everything which has brought her to this place.

Now, if I'd only said yes in the first place none of this would be happening. Yet the reason I said no still remains, fear. What will Geoffrey think when I tell him about Bertie? Will he stop looking at me with pure love? Will his ardor pale in the face of my sin? Or is he more than that? And if God has truly given me permission to love him, then surely God wants me to stop this betrothal of convenience – for surely that's all it can be?

Do I deserve him?

Has he fallen in love with, what was her name? Daphnia.

But I laid down a fleece, and God answered that fleece, miraculously.

I am a new creation after all, that's what Miss Jones told me.

Faith got up and started pacing the floor in front of the fire.

I've got to stop him.

I trust God. I believe He answered my prayer.

Yet, Geoffrey might turn me away. I may be too late.

What does it matter? I have to try.

How undeserving of love would I be if I didn't at least try?

If I could see beforehand that Geoffrey still loved me at the end of telling him everything, would I be trusting God? Isn't it the fact that I don't know the outcome that makes this journey one of trust and faith?

After putting her cape on, warmed and dried from the fire, she pulls on the borrowed gloves. She will return them as soon as she can. *When I go to give my apologies.*

She looks out of the window and takes a deep breath. It is still snowing, but not too heavily. If she sticks to the path, when the coach comes along she will be able to wave it down. But she has to leave. She can't delay any longer on the off chance that the coach is running today. She picks up the hessian cloth. It is long enough to wrap around her shoulders, go around her front and be tied at the back of her.

She looks at Sally, no point in waking her as she probably would only try to stop her going anyway. The door nearly blows off its hinges as she opens it, the wind's that strong. *Worse than before.* From the vantage point of the inn she can clearly make out the road winding down the valley before her. *Push comes to shove I will just have to walk all the way home and if I'm lucky I'll get the best of it done before dark.* She studies the sky. *Who am I kidding?* The gray clouds mean that even now, not long after lunch, the day is darkening. Snowflakes fall on her face and she wipes them away as she starts marching down the path. *Please be with me dear Lord, keep my pathway sure and fill me with your strength. Amen.*

Determination can carry a person a long way, and Faith is full of both determination and hope. She therefore covers a surprisingly great distance along the valley before the back of the storm finally breaks.

Previously, the snowflakes had been landing on her eyelashes but the soft falling flakes still allowed her to see the road ahead. Now she is struggling. This heavenly deluge is something she has never seen before. Within minutes not only can she not see but she is soaked. Her skirts heavy with water makes walking hard and her toes are so cold she feels like she is walking on broken glass. What had she been thinking? Why hadn't she listened to Henry? Poor Henry, if they find her body dead and frozen he will shake his head and say 'I told her not to go.'

I don't know what to do. Not able to see two feet in front of her, let alone the road, she doesn't even know if she is on it anymore. It's obvious she needs to find somewhere to shelter until the snow storm passes, but where? Slipping, she falls and skids down a small slope, throwing out her arms to stop herself from falling too far. Bumping gently into a tree, she uses it to help herself stand. *Right, I need somewhere to shelter. I'll be right as rain as soon as this passes, just need somewhere out of the snow, at least for a short while anyway.*

"What do you mean you're canceling the party? We've invited all our friends and neighbors. If you invite only Daphnia and her father then she will be sure to guess you are intent on proposing."

"When I say cancel I mean for everyone, including the Delaneys."

"But why, Geoffrey? Has Daphnia done something to vex you so?"

Geoffrey is tapping his fingers on the mantelpiece, clearly upset.

"Do tell me what it is so that I might help fix it."

"Can you heal a broken heart, Margaret?" Geoffrey sits down and puts his head in his hands.

Margaret sits beside him and puts her arm around his shoulder. "I thought when you told me of your plans to marry Daphnia that you were over Faith."

"I've tried, Margaret, I really have tried but I can't get her out of my thoughts. I would be doing Daphnia a great injustice if I were to marry her when my heart belongs to another."

"At least you haven't asked her yet."

"No, thankfully. Although she may have suspected my original intentions, I did nothing underhand so her pride will remain intact. In fact, no one except you and I know of this so there will be no shame to anyone."

"Oh."

Geoffrey turns in his chair to look at her, and she drops her arm off his shoulder. "What does that mean?"

"I sent a telegram to Adeline. I just wanted to share the good news."

"How many telegrams did you send?"

"Just the one." Margaret tries to take hold of his hand, but he pulls back.

"So the one household you send news of my upcoming engagement to is the house where Faith lives?" Geoffrey stands up and glares down at her.

"Adeline is my dearest friend as well you know. I meant no malice by it, and she wouldn't pass this information on to her staff anyway."

Geoffrey starts pacing. "I have had this feeling in the pit of my stomach all day." He thumps his stomach. "All day I have felt sick, thinking something is wrong with her and now you tell me this? What if she heard and she has done something to harm herself?"

Margaret jumps up. "Never, Geoffrey, you said she doesn't return your love so why would this news make her hurt herself?"

"She won't admit it, but I've always known that she returns my love. There is just something that I don't understand. Something I am missing, that prevents her from being honest with me."

Margaret crosses the room and pulls the cord hanging on the wall. "If anyone knows what Faith's secrets are, it will be Cook."

Faith is too cold to cry, but she wants to, oh how she wants to. She longs to give up, to fall onto the snow, using it like a soft blanket to go to sleep on. Dragging her feet, especially her right foot, is getting harder and harder. The light is fading and she knows if she doesn't find shelter within the hour she is as good as dead.

Suddenly, something catches the corner of her eye and she does a double take. Light! Light that is moving quickly across the snow.

"Wait!" she yells and goes stumbling after it. "Wait, please wait." She tries hitching her skirts up to make it easier to run in the snow. She manages a short distance before it became obvious that the coach driver has neither heard nor seen her. *Idiot! Idiot! Stupid, stupid lady. Stupid. Stupid. Stupid.*

Now the tears do fall as all hope dissolves and gives way to despair.

"You want to see me, milady?"

"Yes, Cook, please come in."

Not too sure what has happened, Cook enters the room in a flurry of concern.

Geoffrey stands in front of the fire, his arms behind his back as he tries to remain calm. "Mrs Jones, I am just going to be blunt and ask you outright, do you know of any reason why Faith would have turned down my hand in marriage?"

Cook sighs and her body relaxes as she realizes it isn't anything serious. "Well, it's like this see, I wouldn't be a good friend if I broke her confidence now would I. Surely ew could ask her yourself m'lord? For I tell ew the truth, a gossip's mouth is the devil's postbag, so it is."

Geoffrey crosses the room in three quick strides. "Mrs Jones, I implore you to share all you know with us. It is not idle gossip if you believe the person is in trouble and your intention is to help."

Taken by surprise by both how close Geoffrey has come to her and the seriousness of his tone, she takes a step back. "Has something happened to her, m'lord?"

"Yes," answers Geoffrey.

"We don't know that," adds Margaret coming across the room to join them.

"Oh my, oh my." Cook starts fanning herself with her hand and goes decidedly red in the face.

"Come and sit down," urges Margaret, taking her by the elbow and leading her to a chair.

Geoffrey kneels on one knee in front of Cook. "Can you tell us anything? I have been sick all day with worry that something has happened to her."

Cook searches Geoffrey's eyes and knows she can tell him the truth. "I do remember good and proper like, how you knew something was wrong with our Faith when she fell down the embankment. I can also see how you

179

care for her m'lord, but I'm still not sure she'll forgive me if I share her tale with you."

A polite cough is heard behind them and they all turn to find Mrs Lewis standing in the doorway. "Mrs Jones, I believe you should share the information you have. If you do not, I will do so."

With her choice taken away, Cook pours out Faith's sorry tale.

Hope dissolves allowing despair to seed long, tenacious tentacles of misery, as anger mixes with self-pity when you find yourself in dire situations of your own handiwork.

Blinded by the snow, Faith stumbles through the quickly growing mass of white, already half the way up to her knees. *Oh God, help me please. Take me to shelter, please. I must see my Bertie again, and my mam. Oh God, me mam, what will she do if I die? No, no. I can't let that sorrow fall upon her shoulders just as she has found some happiness. Oh please God, help me. I know I don't deserve your help but I call upon your mercy and your great love. Take pity upon me oh God, don't let me die today.*

She stops walking and holds both arms over her head trying to keep the snow off her eyes for a moment, so she can get her bearings. She knows she is still in the valley for she hasn't been on any incline, but she has no idea where the road has gone, is it to the left of her? Or has she run over it and now it is to the right of her? If the blizzard would only pass she would be able to see more. She can see no buildings, not even bushes she could crawl under. Everything is white and breathtakingly beautiful but utterly inhospitable and deadly. There is no way she can walk to Abertillery through it.

Idiot.   Crazy girl.   This is what you deserve.   Pay for your sins. Despondent to her very core, her legs give way and she slumps to her knees. *I can't go on. God, please take care of Bertie for me.*

Geoffrey, oh Geoffrey, how I love you, how I wish I had told you how much I love you. Now it is too late.

Chapter 18

For I know the plans I have for you, declares the Lord
Plans to prosper you and not to harm you,
Plans to give you hope and a future.
Jeremiah 29:11

Such is life that nothing seems straightforward. Knowing she loves him brings Geoffrey great joy, while at the same time, knowing she has a child fills him with discomfort. A barrage of thoughts assault his mind after hearing what happened to her, but through them all his feelings remain true. He had known Faith was his soul mate from the moment he saw her distress outside the Miner's Arms. An unmistakable yet unprecedented urge to protect her had washed over him at his second glance of her suffering. In all the time since then, the feeling has not diminished, to such an extent that he currently feels sick to his core with worry about her.

Snow has been falling for a while now, and although it is still in that pretty, soft stage the land around is fast turning white. Geoffrey decides it will be best to ride rather than take the carriage. Once the horses are ready, and he has a heavy cape over his woolen coat, they set off for Abertillery.

He leaves Ivor outside holding the horses, and rushes into the post office. He had planned the wording of a telegram to the Carrington's enquiring after Faith on the journey here.

"Lord Driscoll! How opportune that you should come to the post office today, indeed, what it is see, is a telegram for you I have, from Presteigne. Marked urgent it is, I tell you the truth I was just about to send young Jim along to Driscoll Manor to deliver the message to you."

He doesn't mean to be rude, but Geoffrey practically snatches the piece of paper out of his hands. The blood drains from his face as he reads.

> *Faith is missing. Last seen at the post office.*
> *Everyone has been searching.*
> *Assumed heading home.*

"Is everything all right, m'lord?" asks the post master coming out from behind his counter.

Nervousness had been mounting inside him all day. Bile, bitter and acid rises up through his chest causing Geoffrey to charge out of the shop so he can empty his stomach on the street.

"M'lord!" Ivor rushes to his side.

"Back, man!" snaps Geoffrey, ashamed of his display. Ivor quickly takes a step back. He empties all that was inside him with three blasts before he finally straightens up and wipes his face with his handkerchief.

"Water, m'lord?"

Geoffrey takes the mug from the post master. "My thanks." He sips the drink and leans back against the cold stone wall. The street is swaying, its movement making his stomach clench and churn. Snowflakes dance and spin in the air as the chilliest of winds whips them around the street.

Through a fog he hears carolers as they stroll from shop to shop, carrying lanterns whose light can be clearly seen despite the early hour of the day. 'While Shepherds watched their flocks', fill the street and his senses. *Oh Lord, I beseech thee, please watch over her, wherever she may be.*

"Hot chestnuts, m'lord?"

Geoffrey opens his eyes, only then realizing that he had shut them, and stares down at a young boy. He has a cheeky smile and a twinkle in his eye, and he carries a large wooden tray tied with string around his neck.

"Chestnuts, m'lord?"

"No."

"Ah, come on, m'lord. It's like this see, I can't go home until I've sold the very last one, and look at that sky, m'lord, there's a right storm a-brewing."

"He said no, now move along." Ivor bristles.

"All right, all right, and a very merry Christmas time to ew an all. Just thought ew might have a lady back home who would enjoy some nuts, right tasty they are."

"Wait!"

The boy turns back to Geoffrey and winks. "Ew'll want a pound's worth for your lady then, m'lord?"

"Yes, how much?"

"For you m'lord, only three shillings."

"What!" Ivor grabs the boy's ear. "How much?"

"One and six sir, one and six."

The boy hands Ivor a large paper bag full of warm chestnuts. "Merry Christmas to ew and a blessing on your households," the boy chirps in a sing-song voice, before rushing up to a small crowd who were gathering around the carolers. Geoffrey's eyes glaze over as he watches children running about in glee, gathering snow for a snow-ball fight.

"M'lord?"

"Ivor, where does the Cardiff coach stop?"

"At the Royal Oak Inn, m'lord."

"We must go there at once. Thank you for the water," Geoffrey hands the mug back to the post master.

"Most welcome, m'lord, most welcome and a very merry Christmas to you and yours."

"And to you, good sir." Geoffrey feels better. Of course she would be on the coach, where else would she be?

They ride the short distance to the Royal Oak and as soon as they arrive, Geoffrey jumps off, throwing his reins at the groom before running into the inn.

A Christmas service is being held in one of the rooms and the sound of carols fill the place. Geoffrey searches the room for the inn-keeper and finds him laughing with some people near the huge fireplace.

"Sir, can you tell me if the Cardiff coach has arrived yet?"

The inn-keeper looks up, still laughing from some comment just made, his portly body wobbling as his shoulders bob up and down. "Due any time now sir, would you partake of an ale or two while you wait. I have the finest around and plenty of it since the miners have mostly given up the delectable nectar." As if he has told the funniest tale those sitting around the fire burst out laughing and clink their jugs together.

"All the more for us then ay, Owen!" laughs one of them.

"I think I am in need of a brandy, but first, do you have someone who can tether the horses and tell my man to come inside?"

Owen puts two fingers in his mouth and whistles, and within moments a young boy comes running. Having received his instructions he runs outside. Soon Ivor comes in, joining Geoffrey, who has taken a seat in the window bay where he has a good view of the road.

Owen fetches a jug of ale and a brandy and puts them on the table. "Would you like some broth? Freshly made today and right tasty, even if I say so myself."

"No thank you, we're good."

"Well just holla if you need anything."

"Thank you for the drink, m'lord."

"You're welcome, I take it you are still drinking? It seems most have lost the taste for it these days."

"I tell ew the truth, m'lord, I've never been one for drinking to excess like, so I've not felt the call to stop altogether. A little of what you fancy does you good they do say, and taken in moderation is as harmless as cow's milk, so it is."

"I agree. My drinking habit is minimal. However, there are the odd occasions when something strong is called for."

"Like today, m'lord?"

"Yes, like today."

"Pardon me for asking, but has something happened to our Faith?"

"Good gracious man, forgive me, I didn't stop to wonder what you might be thinking. I am worried that something has happened to her, but we don't know anything except that she has run away from the Carrington's household. I am very much hoping she will be on the coach soon to arrive."

"I wonder what happened. Homesick do you think, with it being Christmas an all? Maybe she just needed her mam?"

"Maybe." Geoffrey swirls the golden liquid in the glass for a moment and then takes a drink, before leaning back in his chair, regarding his servant. "I am going to marry her as soon as possible."

Ivor chokes on his drink and sits up, coughing.

Geoffrey leans forward. "Are you all right?"

Ivor nods, and puts a hand out to indicate he doesn't need assistance.

"Is the news that shocking? I thought all the staff were fully aware of my intentions towards her. I did not try to conceal my courtship."

"It is not that, m'lord, for ew are right, the staff have all seen the attentions ew paid to her. It is just that you should share the news like this with me, your groom."

"The thing is, if I marry Faith instead of seeking a betrothal with substantial wealth, there is every likelihood that we will need to sell Driscoll as I won't be able to maintain it any longer. You will have to start calling me Geoffrey instead of lord." He smiles, but his eyes are sad as he truly loves the estate.

"M'lord, have you heard any mention of co-operatives?"

"Yes, they are very good schemes for profit sharing. I have listened to many a debate in the House of Lords on the matter. I believe they are to be greatly encouraged."

"Would you consider starting one here, for us?"

"A co-operative in Abertillery?"

"Yes, m'lord. Some of us have talked in great detail about farming, both crops and sheep, but none of us have the funds to begin such a thing. The monasteries have been supplying the government with lamb since the beginning of time, but times they change and we'd like to give them a run for their money if we could only get started."

Geoffrey is impressed. It isn't that he ever considered his staff to be uneducated, it is just he would never have guessed that they had aspirations of a different way of living. He feels uncomfortable in his assumption. "Land is very expensive to buy, even for a co-operative."

"But you have plenty of land you are not using, m'lord."

"I don't have the funds to hire more staff."

"But if you set up a co-operative yourself, then men would come and work the land for a share of the profits. We would all benefit."

"It could work! Indeed, it might even save Driscoll!"

Ivor is animated. "We should grow turnips, they are becoming extremely popular."

All enthused, Geoffrey is just about to launch into a hearty debate with Ivor about turnips and other ideas flooding his mind, when the sound of a coach arriving outside the inn pulls his attention. He shoots out of his chair and with a quick pace leaves to go in search of Faith. He watches with nervousness as three people alight from the coach, none of which are her.

"My man," hails Geoffrey, approaching the driver. "Did you pick up a passenger at Presteigne by any chance?"

"No, sir. Not picked up anyone since Leominster."

Geoffrey's heart rate pulses with great speed and he finds it hard to breathe. *Where is she?* "Did you pass any other coach or carriage on your way here?"

"No, there's not a thing on the road. There's a blizzard beating the Black Mountains right now. Could hardly see the way through it, but these good 'uns," he points to his four horses, "they know the way without seeing, so they kept us sure. Don't think anyone else would risk the storm. North wind is blowing mighty fast though so I think the worse of it will be over before it hits Abertillery. Won't be long now though, on my tail it is."

The driver leads the horses around to the stables for a respite before continuing their journey, and Geoffrey is left staring up at the dark sky as snowflakes land on his face.

"M'lord?"

Geoffrey brings his gaze down to Ivor who is holding out his cape to him.

"Go home and let Margaret know I will be staying here until Faith arrives, she must be on a later coach."

"I don't think there is another coach now for several days m'lord."

"Go home, Ivor, before the storm hits. I shall stay here at the Royal Oak and will return to Driscoll as soon as Faith arrives."

How can you tell your master that he's not being logical? Ivor can find no words to express his concern. "Very well, m'lord."

Geoffrey watches him ride up the street which is quickly emptying with the shops shutting up early and people rushing home as the snowstorm picks up pace. With no peace within him, he can't stay here. He had to go in search of her. He will go as far as is safe in the storm on the off chance that she is stuck somewhere and the coach driver missed her. He collects Donatello from the stable without assistance from the inn-keeper. Pulling his cape tightly around him he nudges the horse with his knees. Setting a slow walk he goes through town, up the main fairway north, towards the Brecon Beacons.

Chapter 19

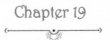

For He will command His Angels concerning you
To guard you in all your ways
Psalm 91:11

No longer cold, peace sweeps through Faith's being, and she sighs. It isn't so bad after all, this dying thing.

She'd been unable to stand after falling to her knees. As the minutes passed, she'd crumpled until she lay curled in a ball upon the snow. *Will you take me home now, dear Lord?*

"Wake up, child."

Who's that? Where are you? Am I heaven bound?

"Come along, child, get up now, this is no place to be having a nap."

Pardon?

"We'll have to shake her awake."

"Be quick, her spirit is nearly gone."

"Come on, child, wake up."

Hey! Stop shoving me, why are you doing that? Leave me alone, I want to sleep forever.

"Think of Bertie."

Bertie, oh my love, I miss you so.

"That's it, good girl, now open your eyes. Let me see you."

In obedience to the stranger's voice, Faith tries opening her eyes but finds them stuck shut.

"Your eyelashes are frozen, dear child." She hears the person take a breath and then feels warmth cover her face as the person blows over her cheeks. Feeling the ice melt from her eyelashes Faith eventually manages to blink several times, until finally her eyes open.

"Arr, there you are. I thought we'd lost you. Come on now, get up before you freeze to death."

With help from an elderly couple, Faith manages, shakily, to get to her feet. She can see the height of the storm has passed over the valley and, although it's still snowing, she can see through it once more.

"How did you find me?" she whispers through chattering teeth.

"Are you ready to walk now, child?" The old woman is beautiful despite the lines and crinkles on her leathery tanned face. Her sparkling blue eyes ooze joy. Though dressed in commoner's clothes her voice is genteel. Although it holds no accent it carries an air of authority.

"I need to get home."

"Evidently, but to do that, you need to put one foot before the other and start walking."

The old man isn't being harsh, just practical. Whereas the woman is plump and welcoming, he is thin and slightly austere looking with a sharp pointed nose and thin lips. Yet his eyes draw her in as they are the same sparkling blue as the woman's. The rest of his appearance becomes almost insignificant, as if the eyes are the only thing that define him.

"Let us help you." The woman links her arm through Faith's left arm as the man links through her right.

Immediately, she strengthens and looks at them in surprise. "Where have you come from? Did you walk here?"

"Concentrate on walking. You need all your strength now as you are still a fair way off from reaching a village."

191

"But…" Faith stumbles and their grip on her arms tighten as they straighten her up again.

"Stay focused on walking, child, it will help warm you."

There is no point asking questions as they obviously aren't answering. *Where did they come from? They look old and yet they have such strength, oh that I could be so strong in old age.*

They walk out of the worst of the blizzard and Faith is relieved that the wind, although icy, is blowing some of the snow to the left, meaning parts of the road are detectable below it. Not having to pull her feet out of deep snow makes walking slightly easier, causing her spirits to rise. Maybe she will get home in time for Christmas Eve? After all, it surely can't be too far away now, could it?

The sun sets, announcing the time as four-thirty, but instead of being plunged into darkness, the moon's light bounces off the snow giving an eerie but appreciated light to the valley.

After a lengthy time her pace slows dramatically. "I have to rest, my foot hurts me so. I have no more strength to go on."

"Hush, child, there is always more strength inside than we know or believe. You can walk a little further yet." The woman rubs Faith's arm, causing her to feel encouraged, so she continues on for another hour.

"That's it, I have to stop. I can't go on." With heavy breathing, she pulls back against their drag forward on her arms. "I have to stop."

"Tretower is not much further ahead. You will have shelter there," says the old man.

"I can't do it, not yet anyway, I need to rest."

The man and the woman look at each other for a while before nodding and letting go of her arms. She staggers slightly and immediately feels the biting cold once more.

"We must go back now, child. Stay or go forward is your decision, but if you stay and rest you may not get back up, do you understand?"

Faith nods.

The woman leans forward and cups Faith's frozen cheeks in her warm hands. Heat floods Faith's body, making her feel strengthened and restored. The woman kisses her on the forehead.

"He does not treat us as our sins deserve or repay us according to our iniquities. For as high as the heavens are above the earth, so great is His love for those who fear Him." The woman's sparkling blue eyes reflect love and her words fill Faith with hope.

"How do you..."

"We must go now. Walk the path that is laid before you, knowing you are a new creation in Christ."

"How..."

"Farewell, child." The old man and woman turn around and holding hands begin walking away.

"Thank you." It feels insignificant, her thanks for saving her life, but already they are fading into the snow and it is getting impossible to see them. Then they simply disappear. *Did they turn a bend? I don't remember a bend in the road.*

Turning her attention back to the path before her, Faith wages an internal battle. She wants to sit down and recoup her energy. Surely she would be able to go much further if she rested now? Yet their warning rings in her ears, and the fear of not being able to get up again makes up her mind. She starts walking.

She has no idea of the time. The stars are still twinkling so it isn't morning yet. Although it feels as if she has walked all night she knows in reality it could only have been for a few hours. Having not yet reached

Tretower, she is losing the will to go on. She needs rest, to sit down and give respite to her poor feet.

A little self-pity creeps in and a lump forms in her throat. *I can't go on.*

A noise penetrates into this moment of melancholy and Faith raises her gaze from the ground to the road ahead of her. *Is that a horse?* The clip-clop becomes as a deafening drum against the silence which had surrounded her all night.

"Shwmae!" *(Hi there)* Picking up her pace she limps as fast as she can towards the sound. "Hello?"

The falling snow is soft and light once more, gentle and unobstructive. Through it she sees a rider approaching. She stops walking, her chest hurting as she pants with exhaustion. *Please God, let it be someone who is willing to turn around and take me closer to home.*

The horseman seems to have slowed as it feels like an eternity before he emerges through the snow and comes close enough for her to see him.

Geoffrey? Is that Geoffrey? Her body erupts in joy and she cries out a moan, unable to put relief into words. Limping, she rushes towards him.

"Faith, my God, is that you?" Geoffrey swings off his horse and races towards her.

"Geoffrey!"

"Faith!"

He reaches her and in one swift move lifts her up, gathering her to his chest and swinging her around. "My love, oh my love."

The relief is almost unbearable. As pain gives way to joy she starts sobbing.

Geoffrey puts her down again, and then in one swift movement he places one hand behind her head and the other on her back. Drawing her to him he

194

starts covering her face with tender kisses. "I have been sick with worry," he whispers, stroking her face, having finally stopped kissing her.

"I'm sorry, so sorry. You see, I just had to reach you before you asked Daphnia to marry you." Faith takes a step back so she can look up into his eyes. "You didn't ask her, did you? It's just I need to tell you first, I do love you. I love you so much I will simply die if you marry someone else."

"How can I ask anyone else to marry me when my heart belongs to you?"

Smiling, she sighs in relief. "What of the telegram, though? It said you were going to propose tomorrow. Or is it today? Is it after midnight yet?"

"Yes, it is, and we should go home and put everyone out of their distress for worry of you."

"Oh no, I didn't mean to worry anyone, it's just all I could think of was stopping you from marrying someone else. Everything else just became a blank to me."

"You will be able to apologize to one and all presently, but for now we need to get back to Driscoll so I can get you warm before you catch pneumonia. I can't believe you are still standing after you have been out here for so long. You must have the strength of an ox, not many people would have been able to remain standing in that storm."

"I had a little help."

"You did?"

"Yes, I'll tell you all about it on the way home."

Geoffrey swoops her up in his arms again and places her on the horse, which has come close to them as they talked. He puts his foot in the stirrup and swings himself up. Once in the saddle he brings his cape around her. Faith leans back against his chest, sighing as his arm snakes around her middle.

"Just so you know, I am never letting you out of my sight again or this worry over you will turn me gray before my time."

"Anything you say, my darling."

"Merry Christmas, Faith."

"Merry Christmas."

"How many times have we saved her now?"

"You know the answer to that as well as I."

"It never ceases to bring me joy."

"Nor me."

They stand on the road, watching as Faith is carried to safety by Geoffrey. Their appearance is no longer that of old people. In fact, the only thing recognizable about them is their sparkling blue eyes. Robes of pure white glisten, as if a multitude of diamonds adorn their beings. Brilliant white hair cascades around their shoulders, framing their faces like halos. If you were to see them, it would be their faces that would hold your attention. Neither female nor male, the same or different, they would be impossible to describe, except to say that they are extraordinarily beautiful. Only their eyes show who they are, revealing their characters, and only the wings on their back give away their status in God's angelic army. Spanning yards around them, their white feathers, tipped with gold, announce them as Archangels.

"Think that will be the last time we rescue her?"

"Definitely not. However, it might be the last time for a while."

"So now we are assigned to her children."

"Yes, all five of them, but it will be Bertie who will need the most protection. The Master's path for him is great and we will come against much opposition protecting his life." He raised his sword which bursts into flames. "For God and heaven, and for all the people of the earth. Hallelujah!"

"Hallelujah!"

Chapter 20

A new commandment I give unto you
That you love one another
As I have loved you
John 13:34

Abundant joy ripples throughout the house. Faith believes her heart will burst from excess joy as she listens to Bertie giggling as Geoffrey bounces him on his knee. Two moments of shyness and then if you want to play, well then, Bertie is more than happy to welcome you into his heart.

Uncomfortable to begin with, the Morgans now all feel at home as the sisters help the staff prepare the table for dinner. Bernard and Nell sip their sherry from the comfort of the sofa while chatting with Margaret.

Faith tries for the tenth time to sneak off to the kitchens to help Cook, but as with each of the other times, Geoffrey seemingly outmaneuvers her, gliding her back to his side.

"In the New Year you may do as you wish, however, for now I cannot bear for you to be far from my side," and reaching out he takes her hand. Slipping her tiny hand into his, she can't help but thank God for blessing her beyond measure.

"They're coming," announces Eva with glee as she bounces into the dining room with a plate full of stuffing balls. Behind her march an army of staff and the Morgan sisters, each carrying a dish of Christmas delights which they lay in the center of the huge table.

Everyone gathers around.

"Well, Mrs Jones, you have excelled yourself, this looks like the finest Christmas feast I have ever seen."

Cook swells with pride at the praise from Lord Driscoll. "Are you sure you want us to stay?" she asks, looking at him a bit nervously.

"I've never been surer of anything in my life, except that I want to marry Faith, that is."

"Aah," say all the women in union.

"Please, sit wherever you like," says Geoffrey sitting at the head of the table.

Once they are all seated, Geoffrey stands.

"I'd like to say grace."

Everyone bows their heads, except Bertie who shouts out, "Grace, grace."

"Hush," whispers Faith, bringing him over onto her lap.

Geoffrey's prayer is one of thanks from beginning to end and everyone joins in with a heartfelt agreement of 'amen' as he finishes.

It takes a while for awkward politeness to pass and for everyone to relax and to start enjoying the meal. Friendly banter ping-pongs across the table and there is much laughter, a lot of which is caused by either Reuben or Humphrey with their 'honest' stories. Faith notices how close Reuben and Olwen are sitting and this brings warmth to her heart.

"I have an announcement to make," declares Margaret when everyone has finally finished eating. A hushed atmosphere follows as they look at her expectantly. "I have, of late, become very close to Jessie Penn-Lewis. She has moved my spirit so much that I have decided to travel to Russia with her in the spring."

"Russia!" cry several people at once.

"Yes, Russia. She believes the spirit is calling her to take the gospel to the people there where she is told there is much poverty of religious belief."

"Aren't they barbarians, those Russians?" asks Cook, looking completely shocked.

Margaret smiles. "No, actually they are very civilized, although I hear there is much poverty in most of Russia. I believe totally that God has called me to accompany her."

"How long will you go for?" asks Geoffrey.

"At least three months."

"You're very brave, milady," says Olwen.

"Could I come with you, do you think?" asks Maisy.

"Certainly not," interjects Bernard.

"Father, I am well past the age of asking your permission to travel. At twenty-three, I think I can safely say I am my own women."

"You're at the age you should be getting married, not traveling overseas to foreign lands. Goodness, Maisy, I would do nothing but worry about you. No, you must stay here, I insist."

"How would ew feel if I sneaked out of the house in the middle of the night and ew didn't know where I was? Wouldn't ew prefer to give me your blessing, and for me to inform you of every step of my journey?"

"I would rather you honored your father's wishes."

"Before you fall out," says Nell, "I don't believe as yet that Lady Driscoll has given her consent to your traveling with her?"

Everyone looks at Margaret. "I do not wish to start a family feud, however, if the Lord is calling Maisy to mission then maybe you should consider praying about it, Mr Morgan?"

"Is that really what you want, Maisy? To be a missionary?" asks Bernard.

"I have had a burning in my chest for near on a year now, Tad *(father)*. So many young people are leaving Wales and taking the torch of revival with them to different parts of the world. I have been praying for a long time now that the Lord might show me where He wants me to go and as soon as Lady Margaret said she was going to Russia a fire burst forth within me. I must go, truly I tell you, I must."

"Then I must pray on it in all earnestness."

Maisy jumps out of her seat and runs around the table to his chair. Throwing her arms around his shoulders, she declares. "Rwyf wrth fy modd i chi Dadi." *(I love you Daddy)*

"We live in remarkable times," says Humphrey.

"We do. Blessed we are and that's the truth," agrees Cook.

A number of here-here's echo around the table.

"Why God blessed us so, we will not know until we reach His side, but I am grateful, so very grateful to be living in such a day as this," says Margaret.

"I have attended numerous meetings regarding this revival," says Geoffrey. "Everyone is in agreement; it started because there were a handful of men and women who sought God's kingdom with all their might. Evan Roberts is the one most well-known but there are others, including Miss Jessie Penn-Lewis. Together they must have stirred God's heart."

"I have only known God for a short time," announces Faith. "Yet I have felt His hand on my life in a miraculous way. I don't just mean in seeing the miracle of Cookie regaining her sight. I mean inside me. His Spirit, like balm to my soul, has healed my past wounds. I fully understand now the Bible where it says *'The thief comes only to steal and kill and destroy. I came that they may have life and have it abundantly.'* How blessed I feel right now, how abundant in love is my life when not so long ago I felt unworthy and unlovable. I cannot believe how much has changed in such a short time, it is almost too much."

Geoffrey quickly moves, and coming behind her wraps his arms protectively around her.

"God loves you, Faith, and so do we."

The End

On the roof of the Driscoll mansion two angels stand side by side and raise their voices heavenwards.

Here is love, vast as the ocean
Lovin- kindness as the flood
When the Prince of Life, our Ransom
Shed for us His precious blood
Who His love will not remember?
Who can cease to sing His praise?
He can never be forgotten
Throughout Heaven's eternal days

On the mount of crucifixion
Fountains opened deep and wide
Through the floodgates of God's mercy
Flowed a vast and gracious tide
Grace and love, like mighty rivers
Poured incessant from above
And Heaven's peace and perfect justice
Kissed a guilty world in love

Thank you so much for reading Faith in Abertillery.

If you enjoyed Faith's story could I please encourage you to leave me a review? Without reviews a book never succeeds and I would really appreciate your endorsement and support. Many thanks.

If you'd like to know more about my books please check out my web.

http://www.tntraynor.uk

You can also find me on Facebook.

https://www.facebook.com/groups/292316321513651

The Welsh Revival
1904 ~ 1905

It is said that 80% of Calvanistic/Methodists churches can trace their roots back to Evan Roberts and Moriah Chapel. Not only was Evan attributed to much of the outpouring of God, but he was surrounded by women of faith who took both the Word and the Spirit of God across Europe and the world. Although Evan asked God for 100,000 souls it is said that the number actually reached was far greater than this. Revival moved the people of Wales, the love of God stirred them and their lives were forever changed for the better.

Left: Evan Roberts Right: Maggie (left) and Annie (right) Davies, with Miss E A Jones

Faith in Abertillery is a story inspired by a newspaper article I read on line, taken from a Welsh newspaper in 1905, giving an account of a service the reporter had been to, in Ebenezer's church.

Contrary to what some people have told me along the way of writing this story, Welsh was actually spoken a lot in South Wales in 1905, many of the articles I came across told of the services being taken in Welsh. I also read two novels, written by Welsh people, set in South Wales during the revival, so I borrowed some lingo from the books because I wanted this piece of writing to reflect what Wales was like back then, and not what it is today.

Today all the blackened streets and buildings have gone, along with the collieries. I visited Abertillery recently and found it quaint and quiet. I would have loved to have walked the streets in years gone by and to have attended the church when the outpouring of God's Holy Spirit was happening. What an amazing time that must have been!

The surrounding countryside around Abertillery is breath-taking. The Brecon Beacons are a walker's paradise, but the thing I will always remember… is how wonderful the Welsh people are. So warm, friendly, helpful and inviting, it really was very noticeable.

Lastly, the main characters and the supporting roles all come from my imagination. However, Evan Roberts and the ladies who accompanied him were very real and their mark on history profound.
To read more on this, visit the Welldigger blog, link below.

There was never a manor (to my knowledge) in Abertillery, only something I am told that was referred to as… the big house on the hill. The inspiration for Driscoll Manor comes from a manor, not so far away, called Treowen House, which opens its doors to visitors. https://www.treowen.co.uk

Thanks to - www.freepik.com For the free calligraphy under the chapter numbers.

Research Sources

For the history of club foot –

https://globalclubfoot.com/clubfoot/history-of-clubfoot-management

For inspiration on the life in Abertillery -

http://www.abertillery.net/oldabertillery/memories.html

The National Library of Wales –

For numerous newspaper clippings https://newspapers.library.wales

For accurate reporting on revival meetings http://daibach-welldigger.blogspot.com/2015/05/extraordinary-revival-singers-1-davies.html

Revival and Mission, Evan Roberts visit to Abertillery http://daibach-welldigger.blogspot.com/2019/02/sidney-evans-in-abertillery-in-1905.html

Inspiration for the story came when I read this article:

https://www.bbc.co.uk/religion/religions/christianity/history/welshrevival_1.shtml

Glossary of Welsh Words

Ach	Disgust
Ach-y-fi	Exclamation of distaste
Anwyl, Anwl	Dear, dear
Ay henwr	Old man
Bach	Endearing word for small or dear
Bake-stones	Welsh cakes
Bore da chi	Good morning
Canmol Duw	Praise God
Cawl	Stew
Croten	Homely name for lass
Cwtch	Cuddle
Diolch byth	Thank goodness
Diwygiad	Reformation, the revival
Duw	God
Duw da	Good God
Duw duw	oh dear, accompanied by shaking of the head
Hen Gymru Wen!	Dear Old Wales!
Hwyl fawr	Goodbye
Machgen I or Bachgen	Lad
Nos da	Night
Nos da chi	Goodnight
N'wncwl	(my) Uncle
Penstif	Obstinate
Poorly-bard	Sick - and fed up
Shwmae	Hi there
Swper	Supper
Tad	Father
Tatties	Potatoes
Tid yma, cariad	Here, love
Ew	This is a pronunciation of You
Yer	This is a pronunciation of Here
was	Is said instead of were

Made in the USA
Monee, IL
27 November 2021